The WEARY MOTEL

MARK SPENCER

WINNER OF THE 1999 OMAHA PRIZE

The Backwaters Press

Also by Mark Spencer

LOVE AND RERUNS IN ADAMS COUNTY
(Fawcett-Columbine\Random House, 1994)

WEDLOCK (Watermark Press, 1990)

SPYING ON LOVERS (Amelia Press, 1989)

Portions of *THE WEARY MOTEL* have previously appeared, in
somewhat different form, in the following magazines: *The Laurel
Review, Westview, The New Review,* and *The Double Dealer Redux.*

Copyright © 2000 Mark Spencer
Cover photo by Scholz Images © 2000 James P. Scholz
Photograph of Mark Spencer by Susan Pollock,
Copyright © 2000 Mark Spencer
The Backwaters Press logo designed by L. L. Mannlein
Logo Copyright © 1997 The Backwater Press

This is a work of fiction. Any similarities between incidents or
characters in this book to actual incidents or to actual people, either
living or dead, is purely coincidental.

First Printing 500 copies October 2000

Published by: The Backwaters Press
                                       3502 North 52nd Street
                                       Omaha, Nebraska 68104-3506
                                       gkosm62735@aol.com
                                       (402)451-4052
ISBN: 0-9677149-1-5

Library of Congress Catalog Card Number :00-133217

Printed in the United States of America by
Morris Publishing • 3212 E Hwy 30 • Kearney, NE 68847

Many thanks to these supporters of The Backwaters Press without whose generous contributions and subscriptions the publication of this book would not have been possible.

ANGELS

Steve and Kathy Kloch
Greg and Barb Kuzma
Don and Marjorie Saiser
Rich and Eileen Zochol

BENEFACTORS

Barbara Schmitz

PATRONS

Guy and Jennie Duncan
Cheryl Kessell
Maureen Toberer
Frederick Zydek

SPONSORS

Paul and Mildred Kosmicki
Gary Leisman and Wendy Adams
Jeff and Patty Knag
Matt Mason
Pat Murray and Jeanne Schuler
Anne Potter
Carol Schmid
Alan and Kim Stoler
Don Taylor

FRIENDS

J. V. Brummels
Twyla Hansen
Tim O'Connor
Jim and Mary Pipher
Richard White

FOR BRONTE, KRISTA, AND DAVID

MARK SPENCER

The WEARY MOTEL

One

When Jo Rene finally gets her car to start, she guns the engine. It roars, squeals, the whole car trembling. As she pulls the gear-shift lever down into reverse, she looks up through the dirt-streaked windshield at the door of the motel's office, where she thumb tacked a note telling her brother she would be back by noon to finish the cleaning and to spray for bugs.

Her car is a boxy Ford wagon the color of a bruised, overripe banana, the ugliest car in the world, she believes, the kind of car an Amish person would have if the Amish were allowed to drive, except that it would be black and clean like their buggies. Around Steubenville, northeast of here, she has seen Amish on the roads causing traffic jams, their horses trotting along with blinders on, the somber Amish erect on their buggy seats. Their lives seem so simple, so safe. Probably worth the sacrifices, the blandness, not even buttons on their clothes. They don't care who Elvis was or dream of being movie stars, like certain people Jo Rene knows. They don't cheat people out of money or steal children. They don't cheat on their girlfriends. Their families are close and whole. They marry and stay married. Faith in God. Rigid about peace. A safe life. They surely have peace of mind. Who needs a TV or a refrigerator anyway.

At the edge of the motel's gravel parking lot, Jo Rene looks left and right, left and right. With the blind curve the motel sits on there's no way to tell whether something is coming. You

just hope you're lucky. Every time you pull out and make it, some
more of your luck is used up, she figures. Even Amish buggies get
plowed into by speeders and drunks.

Route 7 is a two-lane with big trees close, so it's like
driving through a tunnel. Then all of a sudden you're out, the sky
gray and pressing down, snow flakes now sticking to the windshield, and there's the Appalachian highway and a sign with an
arrow and the words "WEARY? WEARY MOTEL—ONE MILE."
A huge new billboard, bright red and white and blue, hovers over
it, advertising the Red Roof Inn twenty miles farther east. Another billboard, about a hundred yards down the highway, adver-
tises the Bob Evans restaurant where guests at the Red Roof can
get a good meal. If guests at The Weary get hungry, all her
brother, Dill, has to offer are peanut-butter crackers and Fritos.

The highway is full of potholes and busy with speeding
semis, pickups, and trucks towing trailer houses that take up a
lane and a half. Jo Rene sometimes follows a trailer house for
miles, afraid to pass, imagining the thing whipping sideways and
knocking her to Kingdom Come.

On the other side of the highway, Route 7 continues for
another half mile into Peebles and becomes Main Street. Jo Rene
squints one way, then the other. Her car shudders in the wake of a
tractor trailer doing about eighty. Her engine coughs. Red lights
flash on the dashboard. She has to press the gas while keeping
her other foot on the brake so that the motor doesn't die.

Finally, there's only an old pickup coming. She waits,
then realizes she could have made it across. To make things
worse, the pickup turns onto Route 7 going into Peebles so that
when Jo Rene crosses the highway she has to poke along behind
it. It has D O D G E pressed into the metal of its rusty tailgate.
The white-haired woman hunched over the steering wheel makes
Jo Rene think of her grandmother.

Jo Rene has lived in her grandmother's house the past six
years. A little more than a year ago, on Halloween, she and Dill
had to move their grandmother to the retirement home over in
Brown County. All the residents were in the recreation room,
shuffling around or sitting twisted in wheel chairs, eating orange
cookies and drinking apple cider, dressed up as witches, wizards,
vampires, and ghosts. Grandma thought her only two grandchil-

dren had escorted her to Hell. She cried and begged them not to leave her. Jo Rene cried, too. It was worse than Kari's first day at kindergarten. Kari had been fine about starting school, but Jo Rene was a wreck about her baby growing up. A big black nurse wearing a Groucho Marx nose, glasses, and mustache patted Grandma's shoulders and said, "Now why don't you have some pumpkin pie, Miss Jenkins. You're gonna like it here."

Grandma sneered liked a dog, showed her stained dentures. "I don't want any of your fucking pie."

Grandma had started to sometimes forget who people were, including Jo Rene and Dill. She started wandering off into the woods, and Jo Rene would have to go searching for her. Once, when Jo Rene found her, Grandma was naked, spinning in circles and humming to an old waltz playing in her head. "Oh, listen," Grandma said. "It makes a girl swoon."

The old lady in the pickup turns into the John Deere tractor dealership, and Jo Rene speeds up as she passes the feed mill, then the sign saying that the population of Peebles is 3811. In front of the post office is a granite sculpture of a plow commemorating Adams County, Ohio, as the site of the 1957 World Plowing Competition.

Jo Rene turns down First Street, not knowing exactly where she needs to look to find her boyfriend, Buck—only that she wants to find him and spy on him as he makes his deliveries. Buck is a mailman and has plenty of opportunities to fool around.

She drives slowly up and down several streets. This is just the first day of what she figures might be many days of spying. Her plan is to take off an hour or two from work at a different time each day and follow Buck until she's familiar with his entire route. She imagines herself sitting in her car on one of these quiet, tree-lined streets, somehow invisible. All the time on TV and in movies, spies sit in cars across from buildings without ever being noticed. At any rate, she thinks she'll be undetected as long as she keeps her distance.

She'll observe Buck going up onto the porch of some innocent-looking house—all the houses around here look pretty innocent—with a porch swing and a wooden screen door, but a slut in a red satin robe will greet him with a leer and usher him in. Jo Rene will be satisfied in knowing for sure then that he's been unfaithful to her, but she has no idea what she'll do about it.

She's almost as certain that he's fooling around as she is about the need to spray the motel for bugs, although she hasn't actually seen any live bugs, only a couple of dead ones.

She turns a corner, and there's Buck walking down the sidewalk, his mailbag slung over his shoulder. He sees her right away. *Shit.* No escape. Surprised, he halts and raises his hand. His eyes meet hers through the grimy windshield of her car, but she looks away, fast, presses the gas pedal and drives right on by him. Maybe she can deny the event ever happened. *No, I wasn't in Peebles today. You must have seen somebody that just kind of looked like me. You know, they say everybody has a twin somewhere in the world.* "Jesus," she says to herself, and she circles the block. When she sees Buck again, she pulls over, rolls down the passenger window, grins so much it hurts, and says, "I *thought* that was you."

"What's goin' on?" he says, looking worried. He steps off the sidewalk and leans down to the car. He's a big man, broad shouldered, and although not a Don Juan type like Kari's father, kind of good looking. But he has an artificial hand he always wears a glove on. Before he became a mailman, he farmed full-time and lost the hand in a combine while he was harvesting soy beans. His ex-wife left him because she was freaked out by his stump, but Jo Rene has confessed to herself that something about him missing a hand has made her feel secure with him—until recently when she decided he's probably cheating on her.

She says, "I just left work and was going to Kroger's to get some things for our Thanksgiving dinner tomorrow." She feels her hard grin start to twitch.

"Oh."

"There was this poky old lady in front of me, so I turned off to get away from her. She was making me crazy she was so poky."

"I thought maybe you were lookin' for me."

"Why would I do that?"

"I don't know. I thought maybe you got some news about Kari or somethin'."

Jo Rene's chest aches. "No." She stares at the dirty rubber floor mat on the passenger side. Smears of dry mud.

"This is a pretty weird way to get to Kroger's. You couldn't just pass the old lady?"

Jo Rene doesn't say anything. She looks at him so that he can see she's crying and will leave her alone about being here where she has no business.

"What's wrong?" He shrugs off his mail bag and reaches into the car with his real hand and touches her face.

She shakes her head.

"Ah, don't cry."

Buck is always wearing himself out, trying to think of comforting things to say. She hates the strain he shows on his pink face, his blue eyes darting around looking for phrases. "You got to keep your nose up."

"Chin."

"Huh?"

"Chin up."

"Yeah. Everything will be okay."

Really, he's been sweet, she admits, to put up with her all these months.

He says again, "Don't cry."

Still, sometimes she'd like to choke him. "Listen, Buck. Sometimes I like to cry. So bug off."

"Sorry." He backs away a couple of steps.

"It's okay. I'm just on edge."

"Somethin' else goin' on? You really goin' to Kroger's?"

She fills her cheeks with air, makes herself puffy-faced as a chipmunk, she realizes after she's done it, then sighs loud and long. "Christ, Buck. I don't know." She looks up the street, where a blonde Mary Kay sales lady is getting out of her pink Mary Kay Cadillac. "I wanted to see if you were having an affair."

"What? With who?"

"One of these women." Jo Rene waves her arm, indicating all the houses around them. An old lady in a floral-print dress hobbles out onto her porch, stoops, and peers into her empty mailbox.

"You mean with a postal customer?"

Buck is flushed a deeper pink than Jo Rene has ever seen. She cocks her head, stares at him, and purses her lips.

"With a woman," she says. "A slut."

"What slut?" The wind picks up. Buck shivers. The snow flakes that have been falling start to come faster.

"Any slut."

Buck looks up and down the street. Jo Rene's Ford doesn't sound good. It shudders. It's not hitting on all its cylinders.

"Jo Rene," Buck says, his voice higher pitched than usual, "if I wanted to find somebody else, why wouldn't I just tell you?"

With the last word of his sentence, the car dies. Little rectangles on the dashboard light up red.

Jo Rene is stunned. She can hear traffic over on Main Street three blocks away. She mutters, "I don't know."

"It ain't like we're married or you're rich or anything." He grins. "Don't that make sense?"

The car's engine makes a ticking sound, like a time bomb, as it cools.

Buck keeps grinning. Jo Rene would like to slap his face. Then his grin vanishes. "Hey, you hear about that Burns girl? The Pumpkin Festival Queen?"

Jo Rene's misery makes her deaf. "What?"

"Heather Burns. My ex-wife was Pumpkin Festival Queen three years before her. She was from down in your part of the county where you grew up, down round Manchester."

"Your ex-wife Crystal?"

"No. The Burns girl. Remember?"

"Yeah, I guess. What about her?"

"She's missin'. They're thinkin' her step-father killed her. They're draggin' the Ohio River for her." Buck looks away for a moment, stares down the street. Then he turns back to Jo Rene. "Heather Burns was a real looker."

Jo Rene frowns. Snow is piling up on top of Buck's mailman's cap. "Buck, are you sure you're not cheating on me?"

Two

When Jo Rene gets back to the motel, her brother is there. She wants to spray the rooms for bugs and finish her other work so that she can go home and take a nap, but Dill wants her to watch him set up some hideous window display in the motel's office. It's a plastic naked woman with blue lights in her eyes, red ones in her big round mouth, and green ones in her torpedo-like breasts. When guests come inside the office to register they'll get to see the rosy glow of her behind. Jo Rene is sure Buck would like it. Dill says, "If nothin' else, sis, it'll be a great conversation piece." He leers, and she feels like slapping him.

"You're a pig, Dill."

"It's a man thing."

"That's true. Being a pig *is* a man thing."

"Hell, loosen up. What bug's got up your butt?"

"Speaking of bugs, I got bugs to kill."

"What bugs?"

"*What* bugs? They're big enough to carry off the ash trays and towels."

Dill shrugs, concentrates on tightening the colored light bulbs of the window display.

Her arms crossed over her small breasts, Jo Rene watches him light up the display. Dill grins like a madman. Mingled with her disgust is a pang of love. Sometimes she worries that he's getting more and more like their daddy, who slowly went insane before he disappeared and supposedly died.

Dill says, "Pretty, don't ya think?"

Sometimes she thinks he grins like this just to show off his perfect teeth. The jerk got all the looks in the family. Jo Rene knows she's plain. She hates her limp brown hair, her thin lips, her broken front tooth, her pug nose. When she was a kid, she had a sore nose a lot from tugging on it, trying to make it longer and narrower. One rainy Sunday about a year ago, the wind rattling the old windows in her grandma's house, she dug out of a closet a shoe box full of photos showing her with all her ex-boyfriends. She cut up the pictures to separate herself from the guys. Then she threw away all the pictures of herself.

She's been stupid enough a few times to believe guys who told her she was pretty. Buck tells her all the time that she's beautiful.

"I thought you went this morning to get a Christmas tree."

Dill looks at the display, then back at Jo Rene. "I decided this would do more for business than a Christmas tree. Got it across the river in Maysville at a hillbilly bar that's goin' out of business."

"How much?"

"Only fifty dollars."

"Jesus, Dill. You could have given me that money for a Christmas bonus. Hell, I'd stand in the window with a light bulb up my butt for fifty dollars."

"You should of told me."

"This thing's just going to confirm what everybody in the county already thinks of this place—that it's just for whores and men cheating on their wives. Or . . . or their girlfriends."

"I don't make people do those things."

"No, you just make it easy for them."

"We get families in here sometimes."

"Of course you're one of those cheaters."

"I . . . I don't have a wife."

"Yeah, but your girlfriend has a husband."

"People need to do things sometimes just so they can feel alive."

"Did you hear that in a movie?"

Three

This past Labor Day Dill took a snapshot of The Weary and had a print shop in Cincinnati make three thousand postcards. In the picture, parked in front of rooms one, two, and three, are the Cadillac, the Lincoln, and the Mercedes of the bank president, the mayor, and the county judge. The men were not in those rooms with their wives. Dill could not pass up the opportunity. It was enough to make a person believe in God, he told Jo Rene.

"Or the devil," she said.

Dill sent a postcard to each of the three men and informed them that he had 2997 more he was thinking about mailing out to promote his business.

"Think that banker will ever try to foreclose on me now?"

"I'd be worried if I were you, Dill. They might hire somebody to kill you. There's probably about a thousand unemployed men in this county that would shoot you for a hundred dollars."

"And about *ten* thousand women that would do it for free." Dill laughed. His pearly teeth flashed. Dill was one of the Warren Beattys of Adams County. The county had two types of men, Jo Rene had realized by the time she was twelve: Warren Beatty types and mutants. Often the Warren Beatty types turned into mutants when they got to be about thirty.

"Even if those bigwigs don't kill you, you've still lost your best three customers."

Jo Rene liked the motel better six years ago when Dill first opened it. It had been shut down for years and had birds and raccoons living in it, so Dill was able to buy it cheap with money he saved from construction jobs.

At first, Dill called the place The Family Inn. A carpenter made a wooden sign that looked colonial, like something outside a tavern two hundred years ago. Dill painted the asbestos siding Jamestown red and put up shutters painted Ivy League green. On the wall by the check-in desk were pictures of George Washington and Ronald Reagan.

For a while, Dill gave away balloons to kids. But one afternoon a mother grabbed the balloon he had just handed to her little boy and turned on Dill. She was a stocky woman with short black hair, and Jo Rene was struck by how red the woman was as she waved the balloon in Dill's face and explained impatiently, "Children swallow balloons and can't breathe." Dill smiled, tried to turn on the Warren Beatty charm, but the woman just glared at him. "They turn blue and they die."

Dill was shaken up and burned all his balloons that same day. Overall, Dill is a decent person, Jo Rene believes. One of the few she knows.

When he first went into the motel business, he dreamed out loud about eventually tearing down the place and putting up a hundred-unit hotel on the site. But each year he's barely gotten by. Three years ago, after a drunk driver demolished the colonial sign, Dill decided not only to replace the sign but to remodel and try a new motif.

The new sign looked like the side view of a horse and said, "The Hitching Post." Dill put pictures of cowboys, Indians, and buffalo up in all the rooms and mounted huge plastic steer's horns on the roof. He wore a string tie, gave away cheap cowboy hats to kids, hung a lariat on each door like a Christmas wreath.

But Dill still couldn't turn much of a profit. A hail storm riddled the steer's horns with holes so that they looked as if they'd been blasted several times by a shotgun. Another storm lifted the horns off the roof and smashed them against the trees across the road. A drunk driver demolished the horse sign.

The sign up now, an electric one on metal poles, says simply, "WEARY?", in pale blue lights. Dill sold all the lariats and cowboy pictures to a flea market. He shrugged whenever Jo Rene asked him whether he was going to put anything on the walls. She started thinking that maybe the blankness was what Dill wanted, that it represented weariness, the desire for a dreamless sleep. But then he put up Christmas lights around the office's two windows, one on the front and one on the side. Then he decorated the walls of the office with black velvet paintings of Marilyn Monroe, John Kennedy, James Dean, Jim Morrison, and Elvis. And he made a sign, a piece of oak lumber with black somber letters: "RECENT GUESTS. ONLY MISSING."

Jo Rene asked, "What does that mean?"

"Well, I guess the main thing is it says they're not really dead."

"Those people aren't dead?" Jo Rene said, pointing at the sign.

"Nope."

Jo Rene doesn't know anymore what the motel's motif is supposed to be. With the naked woman—whose eyes, mouth, and breasts take turns blinking—maybe the electric sign out front should say, "HORNY?"

The Weary Motel

Four

Dill has the woman's hinged butt open and is fooling with something in there. Jo Rene looks around. The gaudy office seems to make an empty promise: adult, pervert, weirdo Disney Land—but the guests get to their room and all they have are blank walls, moldy shag carpet Dill picked up cheap from a demolition company, a single thin blanket on a bed with ruined springs—and bugs.

"I've got to spray those bugs."

"You're crazy. There ain't no bugs." Dill snaps the woman's butt closed and stands up.

Jo Rene goes around behind the check-in desk and picks up the tank of bug stray. "It's cold outside, and they're coming in."

"Hey, you should have seen the mess down by the bridge going across to Maysville. Police, fire department. Draggin' the river for some girl."

"I heard." Before she gets to the door, Dill's daughter rattles up in her clunky old Gremlin. One headlight is missing. The black hole makes the car look evil, demon possessed or something, and Jo Rene tries to remember what movie she gets this idea from. Dawnell has decorated the trunk lid with a bumper sticker, placed a little cock-eyed, that says, "Don't like my driving? Call 1-800-EAT-SHIT."

Dawnell heaves her bulk out and lumbers into the office.

She blocks the door, trapping Jo Rene, who fantasizes about spraying her. Dawnell's fat face glows red, blue, and green from the naked woman's lights.

Dill says, "Hi, hon. You're out of school early, aren't you?"

"I told them I was sick."

Jo Rene says, "Does that mean you won't help me clean today?"

Dawnell has creepy light-blue eyes. Jo Rene thinks they look like the kind of eyes a blind person might have. Those eyes look at Jo Rene for a second, then slide away.

"How you sick, hon?" Dill asks. "What hurts?"

Dawnell is sixteen. Dill had just turned seventeen when she was born. Like Dill, the girl's mother (who died in a car wreck fifteen years ago) was good looking, but Dawnell weighs over two hundred pounds and has a rough complexion as if she spent her days walking into sand storms. She's squinting at the naked woman and says, "This is disgusting, *Dill*." She emphasizes "Dill" because she knows he'd like her to call him "Daddy."

Dill blushes. "Oh, that thing's just supposed to be a joke."

Dawnell takes a cigarette out of the pocket of her man's flannel shirt and stabs it into the corner of her mouth. It wags as she says, "There's laws, you know. Sheriff's gonna throw you in jail for public display of somethin' obscene."

Jo Rene thinks the phrase "public display" sounds right, like something you hear on the news, but the last part of Dawnell's sentence is wrong. Dawnell is dumb. Dumb and ugly both. Poor Dill.

Jo Rene mutters, "Why hasn't he arrested *you* yet?"

Dawnell's pale eyes graze over Jo Rene's face, then out the window. There's no traffic on the road, which is dangerously dusted with snow. Across the road are woods. The motel is surrounded by woods.

Jo Rene takes a deep breath, thinks of apologizing. She recently decided to take responsibility for trying to fix the whole family. Family is important—more important than anything. She understands Dill's love for his daughter despite what Dawnell is. Jo Rene says, "I was telling your dad the same thing about his new decoration. You're right." Jo Rene hangs her head so that she's looking at the hole in her right sneaker. Her little toe is exposed. She thinks how she needs some boots. Then for some reason she's remembering a time when she used to paint her toe nails—years ago, when she was Dawnell's age.

Dawnell keeps staring out at the road. "Yeah," she mutters, her cigarette still in her mouth, unlit. Then she mutters, "Bitch."

THE WEARY MOTEL

Five

Jo Rene heads on out, pushing past Dawnell, lugging her tank of poison. In room one, she finds a used French tickler, a glow-in-the-dark pink one, in the sink. She lays her hand on her stomach, makes a face in the mirror. She'll wait to get the rubber out of the sink.

When she was little, her family lived in Manchester, just a block from the Ohio River's banks, which were always littered with condoms left by teen-agers who had sex behind bushes in the mud. Walking along River Road to Sunday school, she sometimes witnessed the mysterious sight of panties hanging from low tree branches. When Jo Rene was seven a girl at school explained that rubbers were full of babies. Jo Rene got it into her head that babies crawled out of the things and wandered around, that rubbers were where orphans came from.

She doesn't see any bugs but sprays along all the baseboards, then stumbles outside into the snow, coughing and gagging, wondering how many brain cells she just killed and when the cancer from this stuff will take hold. But it's her job to help Dill keep the motel up, and she's certain the bugs are trying to bring this place to its final ruin.

*

After she finishes spraying, Jo Rene cleans the rooms.

Down on floors to scrub toilets and tubs, she wears pads to save her knees and jeans. Ugly stains have formed on the enamel, and there's nothing you can do about it. She uses two sticks to pick up the French tickler in room one like a noodle between chopsticks and drops it in the big metal garbage can she drags from room to room.

With the cleaning done, she carries the garbage can around to the back, through the weeds Dill seldom mows down, to the trash dump in the cleared space between the back of the motel and the beginning of the woods. The heavy garbage can has developed the muscles in her thin arms and shoulders, muscles she never wanted. Her life is full of things she never wanted. And missing a few things she desperately desires.

Dill occasionally sets fire to the garbage, but of course not all of it burns. There are blackened tin cans, blackened beer bottles, blackened wire clothes hangers, blackened mattress springs, and half-melted jugs, combs, and cups. The motel's guests make messes, leave things behind, break stuff. These charred corpses of metal and plastic give off an acrid smell that makes Jo Rene choke.

She turns the garbage can up-side down and shakes it, grunting, then dodges away from the sliding mound of trash. She stands back and looks at the dump, then at the back of the motel, the yellow paint cracked and flaking off (Dill has never bothered to paint the back), then at the bare trees on the fringe of the woods, the woods black and frightening and alive with soulless creatures and the wind. Dill has talked of some day clearing ground for a swimming pool, but the woods gets closer and closer to the motel each year.

"Ah, shit," she says aloud, looking down at mud and ashes. Tears are coming. They are endless—the thing the body is best at making.

Kari has been missing for five months. In January she will be eight. Born during a blizzard. And Jo Rene swears the storm entered her baby's soul. Kari—a trial, a test, a burden. But more precious than anything. Stolen by Kari's father, a guy named Scott, who never married Jo Rene—not that she wanted him to anymore after she came to her senses last spring. For nearly eight years, Jo Rene and Scott had had an on-again-off-again relationship.

"Okay, so it took me eight years, but I did finally get smart," she told Dill last Easter. "I'm just slow. I like to be tortured. I don't know. I hate the son of a bitch. I'm through with him."

"That's what you said seven and a half years ago."

"I was only nineteen. I'm mature now."

"And you said it five years ago."

"Shut up, Dill."

"And three years ago."

"Shut up, asshole."

"And one year ago."

"He'd keep coming back and telling me he needed me."

"And six months ago."

"I'm going to start dating that Buck guy with the one hand, and I don't care what Scott thinks."

"And three months ago."

"I told you to shut up, Dill. Besides, who are you to talk? You're madly in love with a married lady dentist that drilled holes through your teeth because you went camping with that girl that works at the Love's Quick Stop. So don't give me a hard time."

And Dill did shut up. He grinned, showing off his capped teeth.

Jo Rene explains to everyone that the basis of her and Scott's relationship was simple: she was stupid, and he was good looking; she was good at being hurt, and he was good at inflicting pain.

But she never dreamed he would steal Kari. He never really wanted Kari. He'd come to the house and play with Kari pretty often when he wasn't on the road, but he stole her only because he wanted to get back at Jo Rene for finally getting over him and taking up with Buck. Scott screwed everything that looked remotely female, but when he returned to Adams County after a six-week gig at a nightclub in Virginia and she told him she had started seeing somebody else, he said, "You can't go out with that Buck guy. You're turning into a real slut, and I can tell you right now I don't want any sluts."

"You going to marry me?"

"What the hell does that have to do with anything? And

another thing. I don't want some one-handed man hanging around my daughter."

Jo Rene had always felt like a piece of property Scott seldom visited but on which he had posted dozens of no-trespassing signs.

Kari was enchanted with Scott—another dumb female. Kari was convinced that Scott really was the star he made himself out to be—actor, singer, impersonator—and was certain that she too was destined for stardom. She constantly begged Jo Rene to move to Hollywood. Jo Rene would laugh and tell her she'd get over it. Scott told Kari he'd take her to Hollywood some day and they'd both be movie stars. Kari planned to be in *Home Alone III*, *Kindergarten Cop II*, *Problem Child III*. Jo Rene one time told her she'd be perfect for that last one. That and *The Exorcist Part V*. She was a little demon. Sometimes.

But Jo Rene loves Kari more than she thought she could ever love anybody.

Jo Rene told her mom that she would die for Kari. Mom gave her a funny look and said she never felt that way about her and Dill.

"I mean, I never wanted to die for a *guy*," Jo Rene said. "I mean, I never cared that much for a guy. But I do for Kari."

"You sure been crazy about that Scott character long enough."

"Maybe. I thought I was, I guess. But I never was willing to die for him. Maybe be mutilated, but never die."

Kari loved to brag to the other kids in kindergarten about her dad. At The Kountry Klub nightclub in Brown County, Scott used to be an Elvis impersonator, but he got replaced after a few months by a female country singer with breast implants and a blonde wig.

Jo Rene told the sheriff's office to look for Scott and Kari in Hollywood. Scott was actually full enough of himself to go out there and expect to be discovered as the next Tom Cruise. But in five months, the police have come up with nothing. Jo Rene doesn't believe they're trying very hard.

Yesterday, something strange happened. Jo Rene forgot about Kari. She went for more than an hour without thinking of her. She and Buck were watching a marathon of "Andy Griffith

Show" reruns, and she couldn't stop laughing. When a commercial came on, she turned her head and kissed Buck without thinking about it, kissed him in a way she hadn't kissed him in months. She and Buck have made love seldom in the months since Kari disappeared, and it hasn't been good. Jo Rene just can't be like people in movies who always want sex right after horrible things—corpses all around and the hero and heroine are hot to trot. The women always love some guy who's good at killing. Real people, in the middle of something bad, think about sex last. At least Jo Rene does. Sex seems so unimportant, so inappropriate, like throwing a party to celebrate an earthquake. If sex just crosses your mind, you feel guilty.

But yesterday she brazenly stuck her tongue in Buck's mouth. He smelled like Ivory soap. Then she got up from the sofa with two glasses they'd been drinking Pepsi from and went into the kitchen, smiling again as she repeated to herself some of the TV show's dialogue and dumped ice cubes from the glasses into the steel sink, where they rattled and clinked like bones. When she pulled back the plastic curtains above the sink, she was surprised by how dark it was outside. Pitch black. It was only six o'clock. Autumn had crept up on her with her hardly noticing. It would be Thanksgiving in two days. Then she remembered Kari.

Jo Rene put her face to the window, trying to make out shapes—trees, her car, Buck's truck, the barn—in the dark. She pressed her forehead against the cold pane and imagined daylight, the sun bright and Kari running out of the woods or coming across the weedy fields or plodding up the steep dirt driveway, rising from the valley the road ran through, up to the house, a black gap in her smiling mouth where her baby teeth had fallen out.

But her permanent teeth would be in by now.

Teeth, like hair, continued to grow . . . no matter what.

How could somebody as irresponsible as Scott care for and protect a little girl? Maybe he had some dumb woman helping him. He claimed he once convinced some hillbilly girl that he was Elvis' son and she let him live in her trailer for six months and supported him by working at a Burger King.

Standing behind the motel, crying, the trash smell burning in her nose, Jo Rene recalls how she used to dream almost every night about making love with Scott. Now she dreams of shooting him, of stabbing him, of setting him on fire.

Six

It's close to midnight, and Tonya is reading the horoscopes in the back of *TV Guide* when some old creep drives up to the doors of the Love's Quick Stop in a big red tank of a car from the fifties. Big ugly fins and slanted headlights, a massive grill like a monster's mouth.

The guy is gaunt and bent and slow in a dirty gray top coat with frayed sleeves. He has black high-top sneakers on, the laces dragging. He needs a shave, his beard white, and his big ears stick out and are very red. She wonders whether his ears are hurt, whether they might be infected somehow. She expects him to go over to the pharmacy section.

He wanders up and down the aisles.

Tonya's horoscope (she's a Cancer) says that now is a good time for a career change, that good advice will come from unexpected sources, and that her romantic relationship is about to heat up.

The old guy picks up a box of angel's food cake mix, which costs twice as much as it would at Kroger's. He has long bony hands and thin white wrists. He holds the box close to his face for a moment, squinting. Then he puts it back, up-side down.

She wishes somebody else would come in. One of the state troopers or just a truck driver. She thinks of Heather Burns. The thought of Heather maybe being dead in the river makes Tonya shiver. Tonya thinks Heather is the most beautiful girl on earth. She has often thought that if she ever decided to become a lesbian she'd want Heather for a lover. For years, Tonya has wanted to be Heather Burns—not like her but *her*.

She sees Heather muddy and purple, a popsicle in the river. Tonya knows she's going to have nightmares.

Hell, she'll just have not to think about this shit. Thank God, she works all night—it will be light when she goes home to Buck's big empty farm house. Not that Buck's house is bad. It's really not scary being there alone. Alone really isn't bad, except like now here at Love's with this creepy old guy, not that she thinks he'll rape her or kill her and toss her corpse into the river. It's more like . . . like he's contaminating the atmosphere. Yeah.

Suddenly, she feels better. She's convinced herself now that the only danger is that the old guy will give her cooties.

Still, she doesn't like working here and hopes that Buck will be supporting her completely by New Year's so that she can quit this job. She hates January. It's cold and snows or rains every day. She'd like to live in Florida, where the roads never ice over. Sometimes she shivers with the fear that her destiny is to die on a slick road on her way to some crappy job.

The old dude goes into the men's room but is back out before he could have done anything. Then he looks at the t-shirts on sale that have a picture on them of three toothless hillbillies in straw hats playing a fiddle, a jug, and a comb. The caption at the bottom says, "Adams County Symphony."

She sighs loudly and practically yells (she figures the old coot is probably deaf as a tree), "Can I help ya'll find somethin'?"

His head jerks around and his big grin startles her, his bright white teeth a shock. "You can help me find a good woman."

She gives him a quick little smirk and edges over close to the alarm button that's linked to the sheriff's office in Peebles.

The old pervert shuffles over to the candy shelves and rubs the whiskers on his chin.

She definitely needs to quit this fucking job. This January—god, it'll be 1996, she can't believe it; she'll be twenty-one, so fucking old—she would like to hibernate at Buck's. She'll keep the furnace turned up, watch all the soaps, smoke her stockpile of joints.

And Buck's not bad. He's a big teddy bear. His missing a

hand doesn't bother her. It's better than missing a brain, like a lot of her ex-boyfriends. One ex, a guy named Earl, had a glass eye because his wife shot him with a b-b gun when she caught him with another woman. Earl made Tonya laugh by moving his one real eye all over the place while the glass one didn't budge.

Yeah, she won't even open the front door for the entire month of January. She looks out the window at the old guy's car, lights glinting off the ton of chrome the thing has. Its tire tracks are deep in the snow on the parking lot. February is a lousy month, too. Shit flies in February. In school, she could never remember any dates for history tests, but she remembers the exact dates of important events in her own life. Her best friend in second grade got killed in a car wreck along with her parents and brother on February 3, 1984. Tonya's parents got divorced on Ground Hog's Day in 1985. She got her purse stolen in the girls' locker room during gym class on February 10, 1990. She had an abortion on Valentine's Day in 1992. She tried to kill herself on February 29, 1992—that damn February had just one too many days. She doesn't try to hide the scars on her forearms. She doesn't give a fuck what people think, not that she's going to go into the whole grisly story if anybody asks. She just says she fell through a glass door one time. Or she says, "What? These? Man, I got these in 'Nam." Then she stares at the person really hard.

In March, things usually improve. Her bones start to thaw. In March, she'll start refusing to have sex with Buck, and she'll start leaving big messes in the kitchen. She'll talk about a guy who used to give her orgasms as good as the ones she gets with her vibrator and how she misses him. She'll break Buck's Cincinnati Bengals commemorative AFC championship mugs. She'll ruin his clothes by washing everything in hot water. She'll stop taking showers. She'll tell him his dick is small.

She knows for certain she will do these things. She has to because she couldn't stand to break up with a guy who still liked her, who still wanted her. She couldn't bare hurting a guy who said he needed her, so she always makes a guy's life a living hell.

The old dude comes toward her with a little box of Red Hots candy and hands her the exact change. She says, "Thanks," the hell with the part about having a good night.

He looks at her. "You're a pretty girl."

Her hand is sliding under the counter toward the alarm button. "Listen, mister—"

Somberly, he says, "You should get out of this place."

She nods and watches him walk out. He looks up at the sky before he gets into his car. His tongue flicks out, maybe to catch a snow flake.

Yeah, by Easter, Buck will be calling her the biggest bitch and slut he's ever met. He might hit her.

Then she can cruise down to Florida, no more icy highways ever, and wait tables, smile at every male customer like she'd love to give him a blow job. Get good tips.

Seven

Dill wakes up on Thanksgiving morning to the sounds of Dawnell throwing up in the bathroom. He thinks he calls out, "You all right?" At least, he means to. Then he's dreaming of him and Lori, his lover, riding white horses side by side through a thick forest. The dream feels nice until some guy on a spotted horse shows up out of thin air, and then this guy and Lori are driving away in a red Jeep, deeper and deeper into the forest.

When Dill wakes up again, Dawnell is banging and rattling pots, pans, and silverware at the other end of their trailer house, wanting him out of bed. She never cooks (she eats donuts, eclairs, and bear claws for breakfast, sometimes chocolate ice cream), so there's no reason for the racket except that she wants to deprive him of sleep after he's been out late.

He also hears the TV turned up loud—the sounds of one of the Thanksgiving Day parades, a bit of a marching band, then a lady announcer exclaiming, "There he is! There's Santa!"

Dill pulls on his jeans and shuffles into the bathroom. In the mirror he looks like hell, his face gray, his eyes red, his hair dirty. His teeth, though, always look good. When he's eighty, he'll be all shriveled up but still have great-looking teeth—thanks to Lori. Or thanks to the girl who works night shift at the Love's Quick Stop on the highway—he wouldn't have the caps if she'd turned down his offer to go camping.

Lori made up a story about wanting to check him for

mouth cancer, got him all worried, and met him at her office late one night when her husband was on a trip. She put him to sleep and drilled holes dead center through four of his front teeth, two top and two bottom. When he woke up he thought he was going to die. He *wanted* to die. When he talked, air whistled through his teeth. Lori let him suffer a couple of hours while she interrogated him about the little whore he went camping with. Dill drooled and cried and begged. Finally, Lori gave him some pain killer. Then she capped his teeth.

Dill shuffles down the narrow hall to the living room, where Dawnell is now, sitting on the sofa, wearing a beige robe tied at the waist with a piece of red yarn and droopy white socks, the bottoms of which are black with dirt. Dill focuses on her thick calves. Her bulk amazes him. She's probably close to two hundred pounds. Her mother was a little thing, and he's lean himself, but Dawnell takes after Carol's old man, who was always bragging about creaming quarterbacks when he played high-school football.

"Were you sick, honey?" he asks her and sits down next to her.

"Yeah. I was pukin' my guts out, but why should you care?"

"What you think is wrong with you?"

"I don't know. It's probably nothin'. Just a terminal disease."

Dill looks at the TV. "What was all the racket in the kitchen about?"

"Well, if you're interested, last night while you were screwin' your girlfriend, somebody tried to break in. I had to put back the pans and knives I got out to protect myself with."

"Into our trailer? Again?"

"Yeah." She waits for him to ask her what exactly happened, but he's still trying to wake up. He yawns. She goes on: "I heard the back door rattlin' and went to the window to see, and some guy was there, and he saw me, and I yelled through the glass, 'What you want?' and he said, 'I'm gonna rape you, bitch.'" She breaks off, as if that's the whole story.

He nods. The TV is blurry. He hears the strong wind outside.

"I could be floatin' in the river with my head cut off."

"Oh, honey." Dill gets up and turns the TV channel to another parade. A gigantic Mickey Mouse floats above the streets of New York followed by a gigantic Goofy. Dill says, "Then what?"

"I told him I was callin' the sheriff."

"Did you?"

"No."

"Why not?"

"He left." Her face turns pink, her pimples becoming crimson. "But he said he'd be back."

Her nose is just like her mother's. Carol had little dents on the sides of her nostrils. He thought that was the prettiest nose a girl could have.

"Honey, why do you think so many men want to break in here and rape you? This is about the fifth one in a month."

"You callin' me a liar?"

"Does anybody else in the trailer park have this problem?"

"Some boys been killin' people's cats. Settin' them on fire and choppin' their heads off."

"But you said a *man* tried to break in and *rape* you. We're not talkin' about cats."

"Yeah, but I'm just makin' the point there's a lot of weirdoes around here."

"There's a lot of weirdoes everywhere." He points at the TV. "How'd you like to live in New York City?"

"You don't care if somebody wants to hurt me. You never have. I remember that time when I was nine and you were gone for three days off with some whore."

"Vicki was no whore, Dawnell." Dill clears his throat. "Besides, honey, I've apologized for that a million times. I was drunk, and Vicki was the one with the car. I told ya, I fell asleep, and next thing I knew I was in Tennessee. I was kidnapped." He smiles and squeezes her arm playfully. "She tied me up."

"I bet she did."

"I called you from Nashville."

"I should of had you put in jail for desertin' a child."

"Why? So you could live in the county orphanage? You think that'd be fun? Place is about two hundred years old and overrun with rats. Huh? Would you like that?"

"Maybe."

Dill lays his arm across her big, round shoulders and says, "You want me to get you a dog to protect you?"

"Some kid would kill it."

"I thought they were killin' cats." He's looking at her three chins and the big moles on her thick neck. Jesus, sometimes he just wants to cry, but he never can. Something keeps the tears from pouring. He doesn't want his child to be miserable. When she was little, she got out of her bed and into his every night he didn't have a woman staying over. She claimed she had night-mares. He'd pat her head and tell her she had to start sleeping all night in her own bed, but he actually liked waking up with her warm little body next to him. She was a pretty child, just chubby then, not fat. She used to smile a lot. Now she frowns all the time and squints, making herself look mean. About the only time he sees her smile is when she watches "Roseanne" or "Beavis and Butthead."

"They *are* killin' cats, but they'd *start* killin' dogs if *I* got one. Anyway, I hate the way dogs slobber." She reaches over to the end table, and Dill lifts his arm from her shoulders. She pulls a long john with thick chocolate icing from a white bag. Her hands are little, her nails unpolished and ragged because she bites them.

"We're goin to your mama's grave, aren't we, before we go to your Aunt Jo Rene's for dinner?" he asks her.

"Why?"

"I don't know. We always visit your mama's grave on Thanksgiving, except for last year 'cause you had the flu."

"Why? To give thanks for her bein' dead?"

"No."

"Do we *have* to go to Jo Rene's?"

"She's fixin' a big Thanksgiving spread. Granny will be there, too?"

"Jo Rene's a bitch."

"She's had a hard time."

"So has everybody else on this planet."

"You're supposed to spend Thanksgiving with family."

"Yeah, well . . . ." Dawnell stares at some girls twirling batons on TV. "Yeah, I wanta see Mama's grave."

Eight

They take Dill's truck. He keeps the truck pretty clean compared to the way Dawnell keeps the old Gremlin he bought her last March for her sixteenth birthday. McDonald's bags, Pizza Hut boxes, paper cups, and wadded-up napkins litter the passenger seat and foot well. It's obvious to Dill that she never gives anybody a ride.

He's thinking about this as they drive to the cemetery. "If you're scared nights I'm gone, why don't you have a girlfriend over. I remember your mama was big on pajama parties."

Dawnell says nothing, just looks out at the gloomy, brown hills and black trees.

"Well, how 'bout it?"

She mumbles.

"What?"

"I'm not a cutesy cheerleader, *Dill*."

"What does that mean?"

"It means I don't have a bunch of friends that are gonna come over and do each other's hair and make-up and brag about their boyfriends."

"What about that Thompson girl you used to go to movies with?"

"I don't see Marilyn Thompson much anymore. She never comes to school hardly. Claims her periods are so bad she has to have hormone shots. And a palm reader told her she'd be dead with a brain tumor when she's eighteen, so she doesn't wanta do anything but sleep."

"She needs to get out. You're her friend. You oughta make her do stuff."

"Last time she came to school she smelled so bad from not takin' baths she got sent home."

Dill decides to drop the subject. Snow flakes are falling again, and he wishes he had put some concrete blocks in the back of the truck to give it better traction. He slows down. He worked oil rigs for a while during the last boom years in Texas and was amazed by how straight and wide the roads out west were. In southern Ohio, the roads are all narrow and wind up and down hills. You approach a curve, and you never know what's going to be on the other side. Maybe a truck full of hogs. In your lane.

They pull into the parking lot of the motel. There are only two cars. One of them belongs to George, the old man who watches the place at night. "I'm just gonna sit here and wait," Dawnell says. "Keep the truck runnin' so I don't freeze to death."

When Dill opens the office door, George looks up from the Cincinnati newspaper. George has on a red stocking cap with a puffy white ball on top. His eyes are big and blurry behind his thick glasses. "Any floods, fires, or fights?" Dill asks.

"Quiet. Everything's quiet. Only one guest. Fella by hisself."

"Well, it's Thanksgiving. The Red Roof is probably mostly empty, too."

"Gettin' cold as hell."

Dill looks out the window at the Chevy wagon parked in front of room one. The car has no wheel covers, and the simulated wood-grain on the side has cracked, peeled, and faded to a brownish-gray that reminds Dill of meat gone bad. "He paid in advance, didn't he?"

"Oh, yes, sir."

Dill nods. George is seventy-five, and Dill is convinced that he's far more reliable than a younger person would be. Dill understands why the McDonald's in Peebles has been hiring a lot of old people lately instead of teen-agers.

George has told him he appreciates the motel job because he doesn't have to pay for a room over the drugstore anymore. He sleeps on a cot here in the office. During the day he goes into Peebles and sits in the barber shop and whittles and talks to everybody who comes in. That's where Dill got to know him. On Sundays and holidays, when the barber shop is closed, Dill lets him sit in one of the motel's rooms and watch TV.

George used to be a farmer. After his wife died, he sold his place and moved into town. His car is a rusty '73 Chevrolet Impala with a muffler that drags, but Dill figures the old guy should have a pile of money from selling his farm. Then again, maybe he had debts.

"You wanta go anywhere today?" Dill asks.

"I used to go to my brother's for Thanksgiving, but he's dead. My nieces don't live around here any more. One of 'em lives in Europe. Luxembourg. Can you fancy that? Luxembourg." George shakes his head. "I couldn't show you Luxembourg on a map."

"Well, if you wanta go some place, it's okay. A friend's maybe? Just lock up. I don't expect anybody will be stopping tonight."

George is looking at the newspaper in his lap. "Wars all over the place."

"Yeah. I sure wish the government would put in an army base near here. Business would pick up then for sure."

"War don't matter to me. I don't care. Not no more. I remember when I'd never heard of Vietnam. Couldn't have shown you that on a map either." He pauses. "Can now."

Dill doesn't say anything. George's only son has been a Vietnam MIA for thirty years.

George is wearing the Cincinnati Reds sweatshirt Dill bought him last year. George is always reciting batting averages and earned-run averages to Dill, who doesn't follow baseball very closely because he can't see what's in it for himself; the players are the ones making millions of dollars. George gets depressed whenever the Reds lose.

Dill says, "You want to come and have dinner at Jo Rene's with us?"

"Naw. You go on. I'm fine."

Dill opens the cash register and takes out the little bit of money in there. He puts a ten-dollar bill on the desk. "Here's a

Thanksgiving bonus."

"You keep it," George says. "Buy your little girl something."

Dill leaves it. "I guess I better go. Dawnell's waitin' on
me." He looks around the office—the paintings on black velvet,
the sign saying "ONLY MISSING."

George has taken a coat from the lost-and-found box and
hung it on the shoulders of the naked woman in the front window.

Nine

Dill and Dawnell stand at Carol's grave. Tiny ice crystals are accumulating on the black shoulders of Dawnell's coat and in her hair, which keeps whipping across her face. For a moment, Dill studies Dawnell's small beautiful ear.

The tombstone is plain. Just Carol's name and the dates: May 4, 1963, and June 2, 1980. Carol was dead before Dawnell could crawl.

Dawnell has brought plastic flowers and jams them into the ground about where Carol's heart would be. Now, staring at the grave, Dawnell says, "I guess she's all rotted and full of maggots."

Dill is startled. "No point in thinking about something like that."

Dawnell shrugs.

Dill thinks about what Carol looked like. He remembers best the way she looked the summer he got her pregnant. Naked on her sister's water bed, she was tanned a deep cocoa, except for her small breasts and narrow strips on her hips and the smooth hills of her little butt, white as the coconut in a Mounds candy bar.

They were both sixteen, and Carol baby-sat her sister's kid all summer. Her sister was eighteen and waited tables. Dill worked nights as an orderly at the county hospital. Even before Carol got pregnant, he had made up his mind that he wasn't going back to school in the fall, that he was going to get married. He spent all day at Carol's sister's. They sunbathed while the two-year-old played in the yard. When the kid took a nap, they made love on the water bed.

Dawnell is looking at him. "You remember how you used to tell me Mama was an angel?"

He smiles, thinking of Dawnell being three, four, five years old, a sweet child crawling into bed with him in the middle of the night. "Sure, I do."

"I kept believin' it long after I found out about Santa Claus."

"You should."

"I found out about Santa Claus and the Easter Bunny on the same day."

"I remember you askin' about Santa 'cause your teacher said you were gettin' too big for such notions."

"I hated that teacher for that. I was only in third grade."

"After I said your teacher was right about Santa, you said real desperately, 'But there's a Easter Bunny, isn't there?'" Dill smiles, but Dawnell is frowning.

"And The Tooth Fairy," she says.

"Oh, honey, don't forget about the bad ones that got wiped out, too. The Wicked Witch. Trolls. Evil dwarves. Ghosts. Besides, you've started believin' in all those things again from readin' *The Weekly World News*."

"Yeah, but back then I got real depressed because I figured angels were bullshit, too."

Dill looks up at the low gray sky. "I didn't do anything right, did I?"

Dawnell stares at her mother's grave, says, "No." Dill looks around the cemetery. Grains of ice sting his face. About fifty yards away a rich man is buried under a white angel standing on a pedestal, its wings spread. Dill puts his arm around his daughter's shoulders and looks at her. Her lips move silently. Maybe she's talking to Carol.

He hates to think of Carol hanging around this cold, bleak place. She used to love to sun bathe. And he remembers how when he was a kid he never stepped on graves because he was afraid the dead people could feel his feet, might even reach up through the ground and grab his ankles.

He remembers Carol's mother stroking the lid of the closed coffin and talking to it. Carol's old Rambler had been hit head on by a truck full of hogs on the way to the slaughterhouse. The funeral-home director said her features were "quite distorted," not something the bereaved would want to see.

Dawnell is looking off at the woods now.

"You ready to go?" Dill asks, his teeth chattering.

She nods, and they turn away, Dill remembering the first time he walked away from this grave. The sun beat down on his black suit. His mother walked beside him and said for the tenth time, "Well, you killed her," then hurried on ahead, her fat ass jiggling. From the day he and Carol had announced she was pregnant, Dill's mother had predicted doom—God would punish them. Mom had always gotten religion when it helped her inflict pain on people she was mad at. Carol's old man had threatened to beat the shit out of Dill, but Dill and Carol were actually happy about having a baby. Carol's mom just cried when she learned about the pregnancy. Just cried when Carol died.

Dill sighs, thinking about having to see his mother today. Then he'll have to see her on Christmas, too.

As he and Dawnell approach the truck, which is covered now with a glaze of ice, she says, "I got something I got to tell you."

"What?"

She doesn't say anything.

"I'm all ears." They get in the truck, and when Dill starts it, it backfires. He grinds the gear shift into reverse and turns around carefully so as not to run over any graves.

Dawnell finally says, "It's real serious, and you'll probably get mad."

"How mad?"

"*Real* mad."

Dill sighs. "Are you gonna tell me again how you know for sure you're a reincarnation of Martha Washington and need to take a trip to Mt. Vernon?"

"You always make fun . . . . There was a woman on *Unsolved Mysteries* that knew all kinds of stuff about a girl that drowned herself eighty years ago, and there's no way this woman could of known all the stuff unless she was reincarnated. Marilyn

Thompson said the palm reader told her she's a real old soul and
been reincarnated forty-six times and has four more lives of
suffering to go through before she has an okay one where she'll be
spiritually and sexually fulfilled. She was a pipe fitter in her last
life, and you know what Marilyn's dad does? He's a pipe fitter.
Now don't you think that's strange?"

"Oh, come on—"

"Forget it."

It suddenly occurs to him that, in a way, although she has
a lot of nutty ideas, Dawnell has no illusions about life; she
doesn't expect much. He doesn't know whether that's good or . . .
just sad.

He remembers being sixteen and what he and Carol
expected—even assumed. They expected to have nice lives.
Things were tough at the time, but life would get better. Every
good thing in the world was possible. They were going to live in a
big old house Dill could remodel on weekends. Or maybe in a
new brick one. They'd have a Corvette or at least a Firebird.

They would never fight.

They would make love every night, even when they were
eighty.

"Goddamn," Dawnell says, "this fucking seat is cold."

In the backyard of their house, there would be a swing set,
and they'd take turns pushing their beautiful little girl, who would
giggle, maybe scream happily in a pretty voice.

Dill looks out across the cemetery, snow swirling around
the monuments like white dust devils.

She'd wear pink bows in her hair. The sun would come
through the leaves of big oaks and maples, lighting up her face.
And she would kick her legs and swing higher and higher.

Dill pulls out onto the road, glances in the rearview mirror
at the cemetery. He looks back at the road and says, "What were
you gonna tell me, honey?"

"Never mind."

"No. Now tell me."

She harshly sucks a breath of cold air through her nose.
"Screw you, *Dill*."

"Come on. Tell me."

"I'll tell you somethin' else."

"What?"

"I know your girlfriend's married."

"What makes you think that?"

"I just know. I've known for a long time. And I think it's disgusting, and I sure don't see how you can say anything 'bout what I done."

"What have you done?"

"Nothin'." She turns her head to look at the rusty shell of an old mobile home sitting in a small clearing in the woods. "Not a blessed thing."

THE WEARY MOTEL

Ten

Jo Rene wants this Thanksgiving to be special. Maybe Mom is a crank and Dill a pervert and Dawnell a pathetic blimp, but they're her family. All she has. Especially with Kari gone.

She gets up early to put the turkey in the oven and to make stuffing and pumpkin pies from scratch to go along with cranberry sauce, yams, corn, beets, and rolls.

Some years, Mom has had her and Dill over for a boiled chicken and pork-and-beans. A few times, they have gone out to a restaurant. Other years they just used one excuse or another not to get together at all.

She has the TV in the living room turned up so that she can hear it as she works in the kitchen. "The Little House on the Prairie Thanksgiving Special" is on. Jo Rene recalls seeing it when she was about four. Sitting next to her dad. Mom banging around in the kitchen, swearing at her Thanksgiving meat loaf, then coming in and nodding toward the TV, beads of sweat on her forehead, face flushed, saying to Dad, "What's this shit?"

Jo Rene wishes her grandmother could be here, but the head nurse at the nursing home said on the phone yesterday that Grandma has a bad cold and shouldn't go out. This house is Grandma's. She raised Dad here. She taught school in West Union and let neighboring farmers rent her fields. Great-Grandpa bought her the farm when she got married, hoping it would settle down her young husband—he was ten years younger than she was—but Grandma's husband didn't know or care "squat" about farming, Grandma told Jo Rene once. Cows, pigs, corn, hay—nature in general—bored him silly. Unless nature took the form of human female flesh. He was always disappearing for days or weeks at a time. Would come home sick from bathtub gin and the clap. Jo Rene said, "Sounds like Grandpa was a man ahead of his time. He'd be your typical boyfriend or husband now days."

Jo Rene's grandfather died fifty-five years ago of pneumonia. After Dad grew up, Grandma lived here alone until Jo Rene—having been abandoned by Scott for the third time and trying to give her year-old daughter a good environment—asked to move in.

Jo Rene loves this old house, the wood floors and the high ceilings (even though the rooms are all cold), and she loves Grandma's things—the foot-pedal sewing machine, the dark-stained upright piano, the ancient radio that still works with the fat tubes lighting up in the back, the big china cabinet full of place settings Grandma got from her parents for a wedding present sixty years ago.

When Jo Rene hears Mrs. Ingalls announce dinner, she scurries from the kitchen, through the dining room, into the living room to see the TV. She is enchanted by the image of the happy, loving Ingalls and their table holding a feast. It's what Jo Rene wants—"Jo Rene's Thanksgiving Special."

*

While the food cooks and Buck remains asleep upstairs, Jo Rene dusts the furniture in the living and dining rooms. As far as housekeeping is concerned, Mom is like an obese person who points out every overweight person she sees and says, "Look at that pig."

Jo Rene and Dill grew up with old newspapers stacked under tables, the furniture dusty enough to draw pictures on with a finger, dried mud on the linoleum floors, beds never made, the refrigerator full of moldy leftovers. Whenever someone came to the house, Mom would block the doorway, trying to keep them on the porch. If she had to let someone in, she apologized extravagantly. "I've been so busy this week, and the kids just make one mess after another, and I've got this back condition the doctor tells me might need surgery if I aggravate it . . . ."

People would nod and smile politely, say not to worry about it, but their eyes grew wide as they glanced from the dirty laundry piled on one end of the sofa to the half-eaten TV dinner the cat was finishing off to a spilled Coke congealing on the floor to the battalion of roaches leisurely strolling along the baseboard.

After the guest left, Mom would yell that the person was totally disgusted and had made her feel *this* big—about a half inch. She would illustrate with her thumb and finger. Getting up in her children's faces, she said, "It's all your fault, you turds."

When she was little, Jo Rene would cower in her room until her mother's fit was over. Mom would be flinging newspapers and knickknacks and toys and food all about the house so that the house would be even worse. When Mom's fit was over, Jo Rene came out of her room, guilt-stricken, and tried to pick up while Mom got a beer and called a friend who might comfort her in her anger and grief by agreeing that lazy, shameless children were a heavy cross to carry and that Mom was particularly burdened, taking into consideration her weak husband, with a load most women would collapse under.

"That's right," Mom would say, the beer bottles accumulating at her feet. "A load. I'm under a load. I'm buried."

By the time she was a teen-ager, Jo Rene had ulcers, which Mom blamed on the way Daddy had been. Mom told the doctor, "Her father had mental problems and made life hell for us all."

Jo Rene wanted to say, "Mom, *you're* the one that makes life hell." What she did say was, "Daddy was nice, and now he's not even here. He's . . . he's not around . . . ."

*

Finally, Jo Rene hears Buck moving around upstairs. He moved in with her and Kari last spring. He still has his farm but no animals and not many crops, but lately he's been spending more time there, claiming he can't neglect the place the way he has been or it will become worthless.

When he comes into the kitchen, he apologizes for

sleeping late. He has a tie on because Jo Rene's family is coming. The tie, bright orange and yellow and green, is ancient but in pretty good shape. She found it in a trunk in the attic a couple of years ago, along with one diamond cuff link, three pairs of white spats, a brown bottle of hair tonic, and a shaving brush. Grandpa's things.

"You look nice," Jo Rene says. His hair is wet and slicked back, and he has a razor burn on his neck that looks like a hickey. He's had a lot of razor burns lately. "I appreciate you getting dressed up like this."

He flips up the tie nervously. "I don't mind."

She touches his razor burn. "Does it hurt?"

"No. No. There anything I can do to help?"

"I'm in complete control here, I think." The kitchen is a mess of pots, pans, flour, bread crumbs, celery, and the internal organs of a turkey. The garbage can in the corner is overflowing. "But you can help clean up after everybody leaves."

"Sure." He rubs his wrist below his artificial hand. "I . . . ."

She looks up from the cream she's whipping into a froth. "What?"

"Nothin'."

"What?"

"Nothin'." He continues rubbing his wrist. "This damp weather is makin' my arm ache."

"You just go take it easy."

He goes into the living room and switches from "Little House on the Prairie" to a football game, and Jo Rene hears him moaning and swearing softly as some team he likes gets slaughtered.

*

Everybody shows up at the same time, Dill and Dawnell in their pick-up, Mom in the Buick she's had since before Daddy died. Mom still lives in Manchester, a half hour's drive away. She grew up in Kentucky but "escaped," she tells people, "at an early age."

Jo Rene hugs her, and they kiss each other's cheek, Mom's

slack and mushy and too heavily rouged. She's been wearing a lot of make-up since she got a boyfriend. Jo Rene is still in shock that after all these years Mom suddenly has a boyfriend. Dill gives Mom a quick hug, but they don't kiss. Buck shakes hands with Mom and Dill, but Dawnell makes a face when he approaches her, so he stops short and just nods.

"Didn't Howard want to come?" Jo Rene asks Mom. "It would have been okay."

"Oh, he's got his own children to see."

Dill says, "That oldest son of his still in prison?"

"Now, Dill," Jo Rene says.

"Well, it's a fact that the man's son is in the slammer."

Mom says, "Good lord, Dill, it's just for tax evasion. Don't make a big deal out of it. Pete Rose was in prison for the same thing. And I'd like to point out that Howard can't be blamed for what his adult child does. No parent can. Howard did all he could. He even put that boy through law school."

Jo Rene says, "You and Howard talking about getting hitched yet?" She helps her mother off with her coat, which Howard gave her. It has a fake mink collar.

"Lord, no. I don't need another man to look after. Your father was trouble enough for a life time. I wanta do things for myself in my old age."

"Don't you get lonely?"

"Howard's around enough. I get what I want from him."

Jo Rene studies Mom's face for clarification of that last part but doesn't get any. She wonders whether Mom has sex with the guy. Howard is bald and has huge sagging bags under his eyes that make him look sad even when he's laughing. He's sinewy except for a pot belly.

Dill says, "Hey, you know the difference between a lawyer and a cat fish in the Ohio River?"

"Please, Dill," Jo Rene says.

"Did you hear 'bout that girl they're lookin' for?" Mom says. She spreads her hand against her face as if she had a toothache. "Imagine."

"They haven't found her yet," Dill says.

"Maybe she just ran off with a boy. That's what her stepfather's saying," Jo Rene injects.

"She could be fine," Buck says.

"They'll find her in the river, I bet," Mom says.

"Yeah," Dawnell adds. "And without a head."

"I gotta check dinner."

In the kitchen, Jo Rene lifts the lid off the boiling corn cobs, and steam rises up into her face. Mom comes in, and Jo Rene notices only now that her hair is dyed a lighter shade of blonde than a couple of months ago.

"I like your hair."

"Thank you. What's wrong with your friend Buck?"

"What do you mean?"

"Does he ever talk?"

"He's just shy. He's only met you a couple of times."

"He's just in there watchin' some football game and ignoring everybody."

"Give him a chance. Dill's watching, too, isn't he?"

"Dill doesn't care 'bout football. Dill only cares about Dill."

Jo Rene bends down and opens the oven to look at the turkey. "What do you think, Mom?"

"Looks like a lot of work. Don't you worry 'bout that old gas stove blowin' up?" She looks around. "Boy, you got a mess to clean up."

"I think it's done," Jo Rene says, poking the turkey with a fork.

"That grandmother of yours always was tight with her money. Rather blow up than buy a new stove."

"Why don't you go visit with Dawnell? And we'll be ready to eat soon."

"I got to tell you. Me and Howard went to Red Lobster in Cincinnati last night, and I'm still bloated up from that. You think I could just have me a grilled-cheese sandwich?"

"You want grilled cheese?" Jo Rene and Dill grew up on grilled-cheese sandwiches burned in a frying pan and greasy with margarine. Mom always liked them and couldn't make much of anything else. TV dinners were a real treat.

"I'll make it myself."

"Mom, I got all this turkey."

"Rest of ya'll eat it. Where's your cheese?" Mom has her

head in the refrigerator, her big butt sticking out. Jo Rene would like to kick it.

*

Jo Rene uses Grandma's wedding china and lights two candles on the dining-room table for atmosphere. But the yams burned while she was making Mom's grilled-cheese sandwich. And the turkey is dry. The stuffing mushy. The pumpkin pies soupy.

Jo Rene seats Mom at the head of the table. Buck and Dill sit across from each other, and Jo Rene sits across from Dawnell.

They eat in silence for a few minutes. Mom smacks her grilled cheese. When she's done, she looks around. Then she says to Dawnell, "Well, how's school?"

Dawnell is picking her turkey into strings of meat. "It sucks."

"What's your favorite subject?"

Dawnell shrugs. "It all sucks."

"Well," Jo Rene says, "something must suck less than everything else."

"Geography, I guess. We're learnin' about earthquakes."

Dill says, "I hear there's supposed to be another big one in California any time."

"A girl at school says it's one of the signs that the end of the world's comin'. That and all the wars, and you know, there's been more murders than ever before."

"Drugs," Mom says.

"The number nineteen ninety-six is evil, too. We could all be dead New Year's Day."

Dill says, "I sure do like this corn. I think I'll have me some more if nobody minds."

"Bugs crawlin' out our eye sockets and snakes slitherin' out our mouths—"

Mom's eyes bug out at Dawnell.

Dill says, "Yes, sir, good corn."

Buck says, "I'll pass it."

"I can reach it."

Dill and Buck reach for the big plate of corn at the same time. There's a collision of hands, and somehow Buck's artificial one gets knocked askew. Mom's bugged-out eyes have turned from Dawnell to Buck's twisted hand, and she gives out a little yelp. Dawnell shudders.

Jo Rene smiles and, although she had planned to make her speech under better conditions, says, "I hope we can get together like this more often because nothing's more important than family, and—"

Dawnell coughs, then gags. She croaks, "Turkey bone!" and starts thrashing about in her chair. She bumps the table, and one of the candles falls over; soupy pumpkin pie slops out onto Grandma's lace table cloth. Then Dawnell falls sideways out of her chair onto the floor with a crash and writhes there like a cartoon character, Jo Rene thinks, while poor Dill slaps her back frantically. She spits out a bit of chewed up meat and a lot of saliva onto the rug. Dill pets her head.

Mom says, "I guess I should be glad I ate grilled cheese."

"She'll be okay," Jo Rene says. "Anybody want some coffee in the living room?"

*

Dawnell is lying on the sofa, mainly moaning but occasionally coughing. The rest of them sit in chairs with coffee. Some awful cowboy movie is on the TV, but Jo Rene can't decide whether to change the station. Buck seems to be watching it. Nobody's talking.

"Mom," Jo Rene says, "Buck's getting incredibly busy now with the holidays coming up. He says people are sending cards early this year."

"What?"

"Buck, you know, works for the post office."

"I thought he had a farm. Isn't that how he had his accident? On his farm?"

Buck is sitting right next to Mom. He smiles and says, "Well, there's not much money in farming these days, and I need to pay off some doctor bills."

"Post office jobs are real hard to get," Jo Rene says.

Mom says, "You know, Jo Rene, that Sara Perkins next door to me hasn't gotten her husband's pension check three out of the last six months cause the post office keeps losin' them."

Jo Rene says, "You got to take examinations and be real smart to work at the post office."

"Tell it to Sara."

Everybody's quiet for a minute. There's a shoot-out on the TV.

Dawnell whines, "Anybody think I could have a Coke? I think it might give me some strength. And maybe some nacho chips or pretzels?"

"I'll get 'em," Buck says.

Jo Rene switches channels on the TV until she finds *It's a Wonderful Life*.

When she sits down next to Mom, Mom leans toward her and says, "Have you ever heard anything from Scott?"

"No."

"Lord knows what kind of life that little girl is living."

Jo Rene says nothing.

"I warned you 'bout him. Remember? Do you remember what I told you about him?"

"Excuse me, Mom."

Jo Rene goes into the bathroom, locks the door, and cries for a few minutes, standing at the sink. In the mirror, her face flushed, dark circles under her eyes, she looks like she's been beaten up. She splashes water on her face.

When she returns to the living room, Mom and Dill and Dawnell have their coats on. Buck's standing around looking bewildered.

Mom says, "Howard's comin' over to watch something on TV with me."

"I wish you didn't have to go so soon. I'm sorry dinner wasn't any good."

"It was great," Dill says. "But we better get goin', too, sis."

"Bye, Granny," Dawnell says to Mom and goes on out the door.

Dill says, "I feel bad about leavin' you with this mess."

"Buck's going to help me clean up. You go on. You

maybe going to get your teeth cleaned?"

Dill just smiles.

"Bye, honey," Mom says and blows Jo Rene a kiss as she backs out the door.

*

Dirty plates, bowls, and glasses are all over the kitchen, dining room, and living room. Pots and pans soak in the sink. Grease is thick on the stove top. "Leave it till later," Jo Rene tells Buck.

"You sure?"

"Yeah."

He switches the TV channel from *It's a Wonderful Life* to another football game. Jo Rene goes upstairs and lies down but can't sleep, so she gets up. On the stairs she sees a big black bug, a roach or a water bug, but she hesitates—envisioning the swished yellow bug guts on the bottom of her shoe—before lunging at it, and it vanishes under the staircase.

Buck is looking happier about this game than he was about the one earlier. He's sitting on the sofa, and she stands over him but to the side so that she doesn't block his view of the TV. "You want to take a shower?" she asks.

"I took one this mornin'. I stink or somethin'?"

She looks at the TV. A player who's supposed to catch the football drops it. She takes a breath. "I mean take a shower with me."

Buck looks up at her. "Really?"

"I know things haven't been . . . the way they should be with us. But you know. I mean . . . with Kari . . . gone and all, I've been . . . I haven't . . . ." Jesus, she thinks, now she's about to cry and ruin any chance of romance there might have been.

"It's okay."

"So you want to?"

"You sure?"

She nods. "Life goes on." She heads toward the bathroom, wishing she hadn't said that last part. It seemed to imply something final and definite has happened, and that's not the case. Kari is probably fine. She's only missing. Scott is a great playmate for her.

Before she takes off her clothes, she turns the hot-water faucet on as far as it will go and the cold-water just a little. When she's naked, she steps into the tub. The spray from the shower head is warm, but she shivers. Her stomach hurts. It occurs to her that maybe she has poisoned the whole family with her lousy Thanksgiving meal.

She wonders where Buck is. If he doesn't get moving, the hot water will run out.

She has her head bowed under the spray of water when Buck pulls the shower curtain back and steps in behind her. She doesn't turn around. He puts his left hand, his real one, on her waist, kisses the back of her neck, then slides his hand up and around to squeeze her left breast. When they've made love, he has never touched her with his artificial hand although she doesn't think she would mind.

She leans the top of her head against the front wall of the shower, feels a moment of pleasure, but then thinks of Mom snubbing her food. Then making that comment about the postal service. And Dawnell wanting attention, rolling around on the floor like a Pentecostal.

Buck's hand slides from one piece of her to another. Last spring, when they first started dating, they took showers together a lot. Neither of them had made love in a shower before. They wanted to do something brand new with each other. Buck was the one who suggested it, and Jo Rene liked the idea. It was as if they were both virgins, the newness of the experience, the fumbling about. Buck helped her not think about Scott all the time. Still, sometimes, right after she and Buck finished making love, she'd think about Scott. His body, his voice, the way he felt inside her. But often, Buck was enough. For the first time in eight years she could be cold toward Scott when he came around—she could resist the strong pull toward him. And that was why he took Kari. Her baby.

Buck presses the back of her shoulder. He wants her to bend forward. She does this, but then all she feels is a dull pain. "Stop," she whispers without turning her head. "Please stop."

"What, babe?"

"Nothing. Go ahead."

He hesitates, then presses against her again, but the water is suddenly cold.

Eleven

Buck lies awake, trying not to move. Some nights he tosses and turns so much that Jo Rene gets up and goes downstairs to the sofa, dragging a pillow and blanket with her. He doesn't want her to do that tonight so he's lying perfectly still, and lying still is driving him crazy. When *she* tosses and turns, he doesn't mind.

His left arm is barely touching her flannel nightgown. Finally, he dares to shift his leg and touches her icy foot. Women always have cold feet—Amy, a high-school slut he used to sleep with; Crystal, his ex-wife; Tonya.

He thinks about Jo Rene spying on him the day before Thanksgiving and the smooth way he handled it. He's twenty-seven years old, and a sign of maturity, he's starting to believe, is the ability to lie well. Maybe if he had known how to lie he wouldn't have lost Crystal. Then again, he has no idea what he could have lied to her about; he didn't do anything that made lying necessary. She left him only because he had his right hand ripped off by a combine. She freaked one night when he rented the movie *Terminator*. The mutilated terminator cyborg with his flesh peeling and his parts falling off reminded her of what she was married to—she didn't say any of that, but Buck could read her mind.

After she filed for the divorce, she got a job as a receptionist at a TV station way up in Toledo. A few months ago he heard from one of her old high-school friends that she was screwing the weatherman who was on the six o'clock news.

But Buck's almost over her, so he doesn't care. His life isn't bad. He likes being a mail man. He travels the same route every day, and people, especially old folks, treat him like a celebrity or a son. He's important for the first time ever. People associate him with big news in their lives. They thank him for good news. Sometimes they scowl at him (a frantically torn-open envelop in their hands), but in any case where would they be without him? They need him. He sure as hell is on the same level as any weatherman.

Jo Rene snores, her mouth open wide, her teeth glistening in the dark. He gently nudges her cold foot again, and she turns toward him. Did he really lie to her? No. Well, yes. He told her that if he wanted to walk out on her he just would. But he hasn't. Not yet.

He suddenly realizes that he might be getting some insight into how Crystal felt. She couldn't bear his mutilated hand. He can't bear Jo Rene's mutilated heart. Her little girl has been gone so long now. Why can't she just get over it? He and Jo Rene could have babies of their own. But he knows he's being unfair. He somehow knows, although he's never had a child, that a new one can't replace a lost one.

He closes his eyes again and thinks about Tonya, her dark nipples and her prominent hip bones. At his house (the farm his parents gave him when they moved to Atlanta to be near his brother, a rich architect), she has started leaving her things: bottles of fingernail polish, make-up cases, black panties and bras. She almost never sleeps at her apartment any more. In his refrigerator she stores beers she steals from Love's.

The other evening, before the cold weather hit, she was airing out the house, had all the doors and windows open, and said, "Move back home, Buck."

She keeps marijuana in a cookie jar he and Crystal got for their wedding. The cookie jar is a fat, white pig. Buck is big and pale. In a few years he'll look a lot like that cookie jar, he's certain, and getting a woman might be impossible.

He's never seen Tonya upset; she doesn't talk much; she always looks sleepy. She likes to smoke dope, drink beer, and screw. "I'm just the woman you need," she told him a few days ago. She lay stretched naked beside him, her hand on his hairy belly. "I'm just right for you." And she reached for a joint.

He looks at Jo Rene. He does not like himself, but he cannot help himself. He thinks of an old lady who stands by her mailbox each day and kisses his cheek every time he brings her cards or letters from her children or grandchildren. When he doesn't, she just smiles faintly and turns away and walks across her sagging porch and into her old house that has thick blue curtains in the windows. When she doesn't kiss him, he always feels really bad.

Tears come to his eyes. He wonders about the scars on Tonya's wrists. She said something about falling into a sliding glass door when she was a kid, but he thinks there's something she's not telling.

He doesn't want to make any noise, but he wishes Jo Rene would wake up and wipe his face and kiss him.

He would tell her how lonely he feels.

THE WEARY MOTEL

Twelve

The day after Thanksgiving when Jo Rene is finished doing her work at the motel, she drives to Mt. Orab in Brown County to visit her grandmother. On the way, as she passes The Kountry Klub, its neon lights dead against the gray sky and the muddy parking lot empty, a vision flashes in her head—Scott with mutton-chop sideburns and an Elvis sneer on his face. Then she recalls Kari impersonating Scott doing Elvis. Kari was a lot more entertaining. Phil Donahue had a show one time about professional Elvis impersonators. There were children who did Elvis. Women. Dwarves. Black men. A Chinese guy.

Jo Rene swears to herself—for the thousandth time since Kari left—that she'll never be mean to her little girl again.

The name of the nursing home is Pleasant Vista, which always makes her think of Mt. Pleasant Cemetery, where Grandma will be buried some day.

Pleasant Vista is an ugly one-story brick building, a square with a hollow middle that's a courtyard. In the center of the courtyard is a fountain that looks like a stack of children's blocks frozen in the midst of tumbling. Abstract art. The fountain is pale green, and the water dribbles over the cock-eyed concrete squares into a round base where it swirls around once, then falls through a drain. Jo Rene can't imagine anybody thinking the fountain is pretty. She thinks the old people should have angels or beautiful naked people to look at.

The residents who go out to the courtyard walk circles
around the fountain for exercise or sit in wrought-iron furniture
and play checkers or card games. Now that it's late fall nobody
goes out there. The grass and the small trees in the courtyard are
dead. The fountain is full of leaves.

Today Jo Rene walks right past the reception desk where
a woman probably in her sixties (a kid compared to most of the
residents) sits, but the first time Jo Rene came to visit she was
treated like a potential terrorist. The woman behind the desk
escorted her to Grandma's room to make sure Jo Rene wasn't lying
about who she was. Grandma was sitting in a square-shaped arm
chair next to her bed, watching a game show on which everybody
was cracking up over some stupid thing a contestant had said.
The receptionist said to Grandma, "Do you know who this is?" and
gestured toward Jo Rene.

Grandma looked up. "Of course I do."

"Would you like her to visit with you awhile?"

Jo Rene figured that a lot of people must come here to
give the old folks hell, maybe to remind them what lousy parents
they were or to hassle them about their wills.

"Yes," Grandma said. "That would be delightful."

The woman left, and Jo Rene bent down to give Grandma
a hug.

Grandma patted her back and said, "It's good to see you,
Viola." Viola was a cousin of Grandma's who died around 1970.

Today Grandma is sitting in the square arm chair in front
of the TV, but the TV is off. She's talking but not to her roommate.
Her voice is rough and phlegmy from her cold. The roommate is a
nearly bald old lady who lies twisted in her bed all the time.
Nurses come in occasionally and rearrange her. A sack of bones.
Somebody making a horror movie could get some good footage in
this place. Jo Rene recalls that a few years ago Michael Jackson
tried to buy the bones of The Elephant Man.

Grandma says, "By virtue and industry comes happiness."
She has her college yearbook open on her lap. University of
Cincinnati, class of '32.

"Are you reading, Grandma?"

Grandma nods. Jo Rene looks down at the book, and
there's a picture of Grandma when she was somebody else, a

somber young woman, her chin too long for her to be really pretty.
Under the photo: Zaida Groeter, Valedictorian, Polly Anna Society,
Kappa, *By virtue and industry comes happiness*—her quote for
posterity.

Grandma looks up at Jo Rene.

"It's me. Jo Rene."

"Well, sit down," Grandma says, indicating the bed, and
Jo Rene sits down on the edge of it. The bed is hard.

"We missed you yesterday at Thanksgiving dinner. I
made a big meal, and the whole family was there except you.
How's your cold?"

"We had ham."

"You had ham for Thanksgiving?"

"We had ham."

"I cooked a turkey."

"We had ham."

"You looking at pictures of all your old boyfriends?"

"Ask Paul why he did it."

Jo Rene sighs. Grandma's off in Never-Never Land. She
used to watch the game show "Jeopardy" and was a lot better at it
than Jo Rene was. She used to catch herself most of the times she
called Kari "Jo Rene," and she joked about senility.

"Why did you do it, Willy? Why did you bring Paul
around? I had never shamed Mama and Papa the way you had.
'By women and whiskey comes happiness.' Your motto. Am I not
right, Willy?"

"It's Jo Rene, Grandma."

"Ask Paul why he wanted me. Was it Papa's money?"

Willy was Grandma's brother, who died forty years ago of
liver disease. Paul was Grandpa, Dad's father, dead from pneumonia since 1945. To Jo Rene, he's just a picture of somebody who
lived once, in another world, a man who wore white spats and
flashy ties. When Jo Rene was pregnant with Kari, she happened
to ask Grandma what month her wedding was in, and she realized
that Dad was born only six months after Grandma got married.
She'd known for a long time that Grandma had married a man who
was ten years younger, and Jo Rene had always thought that was
really wild, especially for a small-town grade-school teacher in the
late 1930's.

"A black Packard."

"What?" Jo Rene says.

"The first time I saw him. In the back of that Packard Papa gave you."

Jo Rene looks over at the roommate. Her gray, watery eyes are open. Does she see? Jo Rene looks back at Grandma, reaches for her hand. "It's Jo Rene."

"Jo Rene?" Grandma shivers once. "How are you?"

"Fine."

"We had ham yesterday. It was dry and stringy. Did ya'll cook?"

Jo Rene is amazed by the way Grandma can suddenly become lucid. "I cooked a big turkey."

"Good for you. How's that new beau of yours?"

"Buck. He's fine."

"Good looking man."

"I think so."

"Too bad about his foot."

"His hand."

A snort comes out of the roommate. Her eyes are closed now.

"Oh, God."

"What is it, Grandma?"

"Nothing."

Jo Rene looks at the ugly orange walls. On the other side of the room, Grandma's roommate is surrounded by photos she probably isn't even aware of, pictures of serious-looking men and women in high collars sitting stiffly in ornate chairs and of men dressed in the uniforms of various wars: World War One, World War Two, Vietnam. History would be so unorganized without wars. There are some recent-looking pictures of chubby babies and pimply faced teen-age boys with long hair.

"That little blonde ninny. Thelma Lowell with him, leaning against him in the back of that black Packard. Gazing up at our house like she had never seen a house with paint on it, and maybe she hadn't. She was trash. You flew past me, Willy, calling Mama to come give you more drinking money."

"Grandma. I love you. I want you to come home for Christmas."

"I was sitting there on the porch. Reading Edna Ferber. It was Sunday." She's staring at Jo Rene now. "You know what happened to Thelma Lowell?"

"No."

"'It gleams, it's so white,' she said."

"What?"

"Died from an abortion. It wasn't Paul's. He was already dead."

"I'm going to go now."

"He had those black eyes. Right there in the yard in the back seat of that black Packard, he burrowed. Burrowed like some animal that digs and lives in dirt. Burrowed through her platinum hair and kissed her neck, and I jerked when she jerked. His hands I couldn't see. She had a little pink mouth. But he married *me*. My God, I don't know why. Papa wasn't going to shoot him. Papa would have just sent me away for a while."

In pictures, Grandpa is a gorgeous boy. Dill has his looks.

Jo Rene kisses Grandma's cheek and walks fast down the hall. Door after door is open to display worn out and wrecked people in their square rooms, boxes. A nurse shuffles toward a room where a man is shouting, "Dead! They were all dead, Goddamn it! What I wouldn't give for a piece of ass."

Jo Rene strains to smile at the black-haired woman behind the reception desk, but the woman just looks away.

Jo Rene sits in her car a minute, letting it warm up. It shudders, but Buck did something under the hood this morning that he said should help. The radio is talking about Heather Burns. She's still missing.

THE WEARY MOTEL

Thirteen

Instead of driving home directly, she cuts down to route 52 to Manchester, where she grew up, then takes Route 8 and climbs the hills that lift toward West Union. The road is narrow and full of blind curves. A kid in a loud old Dodge Charger passes her on a curve. Suicidal. She thinks of the line from a song by The Who: "Hope I die before I get old."

When she first met Scott, he had a '67 Mustang with some kind of gigantic motor he was always bragging about. He had big fat tires on the back and little skinny front ones. He had a Fuzz Buster on his dash. He said that driving under ninety on a highway was ridiculous. He'd gotten his Mustang up to a hundred and twenty-five on the stretch of I-71 between Cincinnati and Columbus. He admired the way James Dean died. "Man, if you're gonna die young, that's the way to go. Go out in glory."

Jo Rene was actually stupid enough to think he was cool.

Scott sold used cars for Manchester Motors. He showed Jo Rene how easy it was to roll back an odometer. He was twenty-four, five years older than she was and had been in the army a couple of years and had gone to a community college for one.

They met when she came to the lot to look at cheap cars, and he sold her an old Chevy Malibu that had a list to one side he said didn't mean anything. The car was red with a black vinyl roof, and she loved it at first, but for the five years she had it, she learned not to expect much from it, was thrilled any time it started, every time it behaved the way it was supposed to.

Scott worked various bars at night, all over southern Ohio and northern Kentucky. He did stand-up comic routines at some places; at other bars, he sang folk songs and played guitar; at that time he was only starting to develop his Elvis routine, but when he called Jo Rene, he'd say, "Hi, baby, this is Elvis." If she wasn't home, he'd say to Mom, "Well, ma'am, can you tell her Elvis called. I'd really appreciate it, ma'am. I thank you. Oh, and, ah, can you tell her that I love her, I need her, and I want her?"

Mom would say to Jo Rene, "Who is this asshole?"

Jo Rene moved into his efficiency apartment three weeks and two days after she met him. Mom didn't help her carry her things out to her Malibu, but she stood and watched as Jo Rene loaded the last of them, her three or four good dresses and her Cindy Lauper and Michael Jackson tapes. Jo Rene didn't have much to move, and she was getting depressed about having so little.

"Don't come askin' for money," Mom said. "It's not that I don't care about you, but I'm not going to help you out if you're gonna be actin' like a whore."

"I've got my job." She worked at Kentucky Fried Chicken.

"Has he asked you to steal him food?"

"What?"

"He'll probably expect you to steal him supper every night. He's crooked as a West Virginia road."

Jo Rene just said, "Oh, Mom," and got in her car. She was afraid it wouldn't start, and it didn't the first three tries, but finally the engine caught; she rolled out of the driveway, her mother behind her with her hands on her hips, and Jo Rene said to herself, "I'm on my way to my new life," and was happier than she had ever been.

*

She turns onto a gravel road, and after a mile or so the land flattens out some, and there it is—the house Grandma grew up in. It's a three-story Victorian with cupolas and spires, like a castle, and gingerbread woodwork all along the portion of the porch that hasn't collapsed; the porch roof is full of holes, as if it had been bombed. The sun, which is setting directly behind it, frames the house in radiance.

It's clear that the house must have really been beautiful in its day. White. Gleaming. Now it's windowless, the wood the color of rot. The barn and other buildings have vanished without a trace. No driveway leads to the house. It sits in the middle of a farmer's muddy field.

There's no fence to climb, and a couple of months ago, when Jo Rene parked along here, she got out of her car and started across the field, which was thick with tall hay then. The farmer who owns the property came out of his little brick house across the road and hollered at Jo Rene to get the hell out of his field. She pointed to the old house and yelled, "My grandma's house."

"You get out!"

"I just want to look inside."

"I'll get my dogs!"

"I just want to look through a window."

"You get. Now!"

Jo Rene threw up her arms and headed back to her car.

Today, if she tried to cross the field, she'd sink in the mud. As a child, she lost a pair of new boots in a muddy field when her family went down to Kentucky to visit one of Mom's brothers, who owned a squalid little farm he tried to grow corn and tobacco on. The field sucked at her boots like a monster and wouldn't let go. She tramped into her uncle's house in her socks caked with mud, and Mom whipped her with a switch.

Sitting in her car, she tries to imagine Grandma's place as it used to be—a home, a prosperous farm. Grandma's father had money. *His* father had been mayor of the town of West Union, and before him there had been numerous gentlemen and ladies, almost all of whom avoided dying of cholera or in childbirth or in the Civil War. Doctors and teachers and lawyers and rich farmers. Grandma's father sent Grandma to college. Willy flunked out and drank himself to death. Grandma married a bum, a drinking buddy of her brother's. Even back then people let romance and sex ruin their lives.

Dad moved to Manchester to work in a mill and married a hillbilly from across the river and had two lousy kids—Dill, who got married at sixteen and has bummed around from job to job, now running a sleazy motel; Jo Rene herself, who had a baby without getting married and has no job skills except cleaning toilets.

She puts the car in gear, takes another look at the house, and drives away, thinking about what a hopeless case Dawnell is.

Fourteen

The Reverend Elvis L. Haywood sits on the edge of his ragged winged-back chair, studying the techniques of a Las Vegas faith healer on cable TV and stroking his one-eyed cat.

The chair used to be white, has turned yellow with age, and has frayed arms. Its wings are huge. The cat's right pupil looks kind of pink today instead of milky white, a hopeful sign that Haywood's prayers are working.

Last Sunday Haywood gave a sermon on signs. He tried out his new technique of emphasizing important words. "The *Lord* directs our *lives* with *signs*," he said. "We just have to know how to *read* them as we *drive* down the highway of *life*." He waved his fist. "Now I'm not talking about old *wives'* tales, like a bird flying into a window pane and *killing* itself and that supposedly meaning somebody in the house is destined to *die* soon."

He paused the way he had practiced. "So what am I *talking* about?" A rhetorical question, of course, but the Wilmers' boy raised his hand as if he had an answer. The boy is twelve and not bright. His mother pulled his arm down. "Well, *guilt* can be a sign."

Then after another pause, nodding his head, he said softly, "Yes. Guilt. Guilt . . . is God's sign to us that we shouldn't be *stealing* paper clips from our offices or looking with *lust* at our neighbor's wife or *copying* answers off our classmates."

The entire congregation looked bored—the Oswalds, the

Wilmers, the Picks, old Mrs. Foster, old Miss Groseclose.

"Our car not starting could be *a sign* that we should not take a trip." Laura Oswald yawned. The Picks' younger boy, who must be fourteen or fifteen—an age when the devil often commences work on a child—loudly passed gas and hid his giggles behind a hymnal. Miss Groseclose yawned.

The Las Vegas faith healer on the TV has people shouting and screaming and convulsing. She's an ugly wizened woman in a white choir robe. It looks as though she painted her high stiff black hair and then coated it with shellac. Her thick eyebrows arch demonically. What really amazes him is that her teeth are bad, not crooked but spaced and yellow. You'd expect a Las Vegas faith healer who makes frequent cable TV appearances to go to the trouble of having her teeth fixed. The bad teeth contradict the fancy hair, making it difficult for Haywood to decide whether she's a fake.

She shrieks like a banshee when she evokes God's help in healing the people lined up on her stage, and she knocks the hell out of them, her palm smashing into their foreheads. Haywood is reminded of the kung-fu movies he sometimes watches late at night; if her aim was low and she smashed some poor cripple's nose, she'd probably send bone chips into the person's brain. As is, Haywood cringes at the way she rears back and slams foreheads with her open hand, the fingers splayed wide—a loud pop of flesh, the neck snapping back, a couple of muscle-bound goons in dark suits catching the limp body. Then the flutter of eyelids and the discovery that a leg, spine, eye, or major internal organ works again. Praise Jesus! Praise Jesus!

Haywood has a satellite dish outside his small clapboard house. He lives on the fringe of Peebles where the town peters out with a short string of shotgun shacks and beat-up mobile homes. His neighbors' places, unpainted and the yards cluttered with rusty cars on concrete blocks, contrast with his tidy flower beds and weedless lawn. Years ago, in the back, he built a brick barbecue pit. Then he wrote a letter to Jimmy Carter, inviting the president to his Sunday service, to be followed by a barbecue. Haywood was certain Carter would come. He had dreamed vividly about the president sitting on a lawn chair out back with a paper plate heaped with baked beans and potato salad. But Carter wrote back saying he was busy.

Haywood has had other vivid dreams about famous people eating in his backyard, and he has written to them all. In his dreams, Loretta Lynn ate chicken wings; Oral Roberts ate shrimp; Ollie North had steak, rare and bloody; Dan Quayle nibbled a banana. But the famous people are always too busy to come hear Haywood preach and eat his food. Ronald Reagan never even wrote back.

The Las Vegas faith healer is saying good-bye to the TV audience. Haywood thinks snidely that she probably heads for the casinos after her shows, but he admits he might be simply jealous. Like Mr. Wilmers. Haywood has been counseling Mr. and Mrs. Wilmers for six months. Mrs. Wilmers went to the junior college in Portsmouth a couple of years ago and now makes more money as a nurse than her husband does working their farm. In addition to saying he thought his wife had turned into a cold bitch and probably wanted to have sex with doctors, Wilmers bitterly confessed that he felt God let his wife make more money because God liked her better.

Haywood assured Wilmers that God is just, has a plan, knows what He's doing.

But sometimes Haywood wonders himself about the Almighty's agenda: blesses some gaudy phony with her own TV revival show but . . . . His spine shivers with fear. Then his face burns with anger. Well, blazes, he'll go ahead and think it—God kung fu kicks the living daylights out of a decent, hard-working man dedicated to preaching the Word and abiding by His edicts—gives him poverty, a wife who dies young, rejected invitations . . . .

Haywood hangs his head in shame and says a quick prayer asking for forgiveness. Who is he to question God's ways?

He gets up and switches the TV to a home-improvement show on which carpenters are re-plastering old walls.

Haywood sits back down in his winged-back chair and strokes the cat's head, studies the cat's blind eye again. Yes, it's turned pinkish. A sign. But of what? He practices his faith-healing techniques on small animals—he loves animals and is certain they have souls, despite what some other preachers say.

He has healed only one human being: his son-in-law. Earl had stomach cancer a year ago, which is now in total remission. Haywood hates Earl, who married his daughter Anita when she was fourteen. Earl is a boozer and a whoremonger and an idiot. Haywood would like to see him dead.

A commotion erupts outside. A car with a bad muffler rumbles in the driveway. The collie with the broken back and the terrier with the gum disease both bark. The hamster with emotional problems bangs its head against its cage.

A fat girl heaves herself out from under the steering wheel and lumbers toward the front door, as Haywood watches from a chink in the living-room curtain. Haywood is impeccably dressed: polished black winged-tip shoes, black suspenders, white shirt, narrow black tie. But his collar and short cuffs are a bit frayed, and the pants are shiny from wear. The soles of the bright shoes are worn smooth. In the small mirror by the front door, he glances at his thin face, lines etched deep on either side of his nose and across his forehead. His salt-and-pepper hair is slicked back behind his ears like wings.

When he opens the door, he says, "May I help you?"

The fat girl stares wide-eyed at him with her mouth open. She's wearing a man's flannel shirt with a pack of Marlboros in the breast pocket. After what seems a long time, she finally blinks and says, "You're the only one who can help me."

"Why, child—"

"You've got to."

"Well, sure, I will." He feels the holy spirit stir inside him, swell with goodness and power. But the girl has turned and lumbers back toward her car. "Wait. Where are you going?"

"I don't know." She turns back. "You know, I don't even go to your church. Any church, for that matter. But I heard about that guy you cured of cancer."

"Oh." He waves his hand meaninglessly.

"Help me."

"Okay."

"See, I'm pregnant."

Fifteen

Buck doesn't deliver mail out in the country, just in town.
The old man who delivers Jo Rene's mail has warts on his face,
like Robert Redford, but he's no Robert Redford. He hunches
over the steering wheel of his mail truck, wearing a helmet-like
cap with ear flaps, and Jo Rene thinks of an old movie in which
Clark Gable played a race-car driver. She always gets nervous
watching the people in old movies zooming around in cars without
seat belts, without padded dash boards, without break-away
steering wheels, without shatterproof glass. It's a wonder the
human race wasn't wiped out by the middle of the century.

It's Saturday, and the mail man comes early in the morning, before nine, bringing a fist full of bills and junk mail. Jo
Rene stands at the kitchen counter by the window. One letter
congratulates her on being pre-approved for a Visa Gold card. It
assumes she makes thirty thousand a year, three times what she
really makes. Where the hell do people get her name? Who do
they think she is?

One envelope is soggy and dirty with the imprint of
somebody's snow boot. She stares at it, turns it over. There's no
return address, no company logo. Her name and address are
written in a childish scrawl, and Jo Rene's heart kicks into a
higher gear as she tears at the envelope.

Kari. It could be about Kari. It could be from Scott. Or
from Kari herself. The boot print hides the post mark.

She begins to read. The words shimmer like a stretch of highway on a hot day. "Love conquers . . . " is all she gets at first. ". . . luck . . . ." Her head spins. ". . . fortunes . . . ." Then it starts to make sense. And Jo Rene's heart shrivels. ". . . death . . . ." She feels herself caving in, curling up like a snail. She sits in a chair in her kitchen and re-reads the letter.

It's a chain letter, a photocopy, that says, "Love conquers all" and that if she makes ten copies of the letter and distributes them to people who need good luck, she herself can be the recipient of a great fortune. She doesn't have to send money because "Good luck has no price."

She got a chain letter once in high school that said it had been started by a Franciscan monk in Tibet, but this one says it was started by E. L. Haywood, pastor of The Church of the Glorious Resurrection in Peebles. Nevertheless, it has been around the world six times in the last year, "bringing good fortune to many Americans and Christian foreigners both." At the bottom of the letter, there's a strong warning typed in all capital letters. If she breaks the chain, no one will win the Ohio Lotto, inherit a million dollars from a distant relative, receive an unexpected tax refund, be miraculously cured of cancer, or have an absent loved one return. In fact, the person who breaks the chain could get audited by the IRS, slip in their bathtub, or lose a limb.

Jo Rene's face burns. She wads the letter into a ball and throws it toward the stove. She goes to the sink and washes her hands, then turns and stares at the crumpled piece of paper on the floor.

The world is full of fools. She trembles. She looks at the envelope lying on the table. She bends down to it and squints at her name and address scrawled in pencil.

She retrieves the letter and takes it to the living room, where she sits on the sofa, holding it in her fist and thinking. Then she uncrumples it and smoothes it out the best she can on her lap.

Sixteen

On her way to Manchester to go shopping with her mother, Jo Rene stops at the Kroger supermarket in Peebles to use the photocopy machine at a quarter a copy. In Manchester she parks by the flood wall on River Avenue. All the houses and stores have crumbling bricks, rotting boards, peeling paint. All the people who live down here seem to be either obese or emaciated. They have only half their teeth. They limp, and their skin looks muddy and unhealthy, like the river. Jo Rene wouldn't dare go up to the houses; instead, she walks from car to car parked along the street—Fords and Chevies and Dodges with smashed fenders and rusty roofs and cracked windshields and bald tires—slipping copies of the chain letter under the windshield wipers. She looks through the windows and sees split seats, some partly covered by dirty blankets. Saint Christopher medals, Playboy emblems, fuzzy dice, garter belts, trolls, and little statues of Jesus hang from the rear-view mirrors. Jo Rene slips the last copy under the wind-shield wiper of a van with a mountain landscape painted on the side, pine trees silhouetted against a full moon, all of it faded and ruined by bleeding sores of rust. People who need luck. Now it's out of her hands. She's done her duty.

After she drives a few blocks along the river, she sees the county search-and-rescue team dragging the cold, muddy water. The Pumpkin Festival Queen is still missing.

Jo Rene and her mother go to a big flea market that

recently opened in what used to be a movie theater. It was Jo Rene's idea to go to the flea market. "Dead people's junk," Mom says, pointing at a table displaying cracked china, then at a rack of old clothes.

Jo Rene likes old things. She wants to know more about the past and understand it. Looking at a stack of old board games, she says, "What did you and Daddy do for fun?"

"We never had fun," Mom says, picking up a rusty dog chain and frowning at it.

"I don't remember you going out, but you guys must have done something, must have had some interests in common. Where did you go on dates before you got married?"

"Bowling. Your father was a great bowler."

"I don't remember Daddy bowling."

"He gave it up after he realized he wouldn't ever get to go on tour and be on TV. Lord, I should have known then that the man would bore me silly."

Jo Rene does remember Daddy watching bowling on TV. "Did he really want to be a professional?"

"He said he did. That was long before you and Dill were born. He had some trophies, but he gave them to the girlfriend he broke up with when he met me. I guess she hocked them or something."

"Maybe she still has them."

Mom picks up a dusty book, puts it down immediately, wipes her hand on her coat. "All this junk depresses me."

Jo Rene picks up a woman's leather shoe with a pointed toe. "How in the world did they wear these?"

"They were crazy."

"Look at that old radio." The table radio Jo Rene points at has been refinished. The wood is ornately carved and glossy.

"My mother had one like that," Mom says. "Used to listen to the Grand 'Ol Opry on it."

"Really? What became of it?"

"I have no idea." Mom picks up a frayed dog collar with embedded rhinestones. "Somebody had a dog. Thing smells like dog." She makes a face.

"Yeah. It's sad. The dog must have died."

Mom shrugs. "Yeah. You used to be crazy about dogs."

Jo Rene's stomach turns all of a sudden. "I know. Remember Rex?"

"Don't start, Jo Rene."

"I'm not starting anything."

"Every few months you bring up how I killed that old mongrel dog you had when you were ten."

"Well, you did."

"Oh, hush. I did no such thing."

Mom picks up a strange-looking lamp and examines it until she suddenly realizes it's supposed to look like an erect penis. She puts it down quickly. "You really like this trash?" she says to Jo Rene's back.

Jo Rene moves ahead, determined to see all the items in the flea market, to enjoy her day off, but she finds herself thinking about Rex. She used to introduce Rex to adults as her best friend. She kissed Rex on his black lips, although Mom told her she was going to die of some dog disease if she didn't stop it.

Mom took Rex to the grocery store one hot day and left him in the car. By the time she finished her shopping, he was dead.

Jo Rene remembers standing in the kitchen of the house she grew up in and saying, "You killed Rex," as Mom bent down to put two TV dinners in the oven. "You cooked his brain. You didn't have to take Rex with you."

Mom straightened up, reached for her sweaty beer bottle on the counter, and turned her slit eyes at Jo Rene. "You know why I took him. You want *me* dead? I needed protection."

"Rex would of just licked the guy's face. He wasn't mean."

"He was a big dog. They say on the news that's enough to scare away attackers."

Three Adams County women had recently been abducted, raped, and murdered. On TV, their covered bodies were shown being carried up the banks of the river. Relatives stood close by, a woman pressing her face into the shoulder of a gaunt long-haired man, the TV camera moving in close so everybody could be entertained by their grief.

"Now, I like this," Mom says behind Jo Rene. Jo Rene turns and sees her holding up a new-looking tee-shirt that says,

"Aged Like Fine Wine. Pop My Cork, Handsome."

"Yeah, real classy." Thinking about Rex makes Jo Rene feel like being mean.

"Well, I just might buy it."

"Why don't you buy that penis lamp?"

"That thing's disgusting."

"And this shirt isn't?"

"There's no comparison, Jo Rene."

Jo Rene doesn't want to ruin this outing with Mom, but she can't stop thinking about her killing Rex. And that memory evokes a list of grievances. Just day before yesterday—being rude to Buck, eating that grilled cheese . . . .

"If I would have come home wearing something like that when I was younger, you would have slapped me silly. You maybe still would."

"Hush now, Jo Rene Jenkins."

"What will Howard think?"

"No man's gonna tell me what to wear."

Jo Rene walks ahead, picks up some old black hats with black veils, the kind that mysterious women in 1940's movies wear. She fingers some baby clothes. Mom comes up beside her. "I got some Tylenol in my purse if you're crampin' today."

"I'm fine. There's nothing wrong with me."

They move along between the rows of tables crowded with drinking glasses, tarnished silver ware, old magazines, broken toys, rusty tools.

"What do you think of chain letters?" Jo Rene asks.

"Aren't they just a way of cheating people out of money?"

"Not always. Some don't ask for money. They're for good luck."

"There are a lot of stupid people in the world, honey. Oh, look at this." Mom points at an old Barbie doll in a box with a cellophane window. The box is faded and has a layer of dust on its top but has apparently never been opened. The Barbie is wearing a pink party dress. "It's like brand new. I wonder why it never got opened."

Jo Rene stares and feels dizzy. Something is terribly wrong here, but she is not sure what. "This . . . this shouldn't be here."

"Never been played with. Isn't it nice?"

"Let's get away from it."

Out on the sidewalk, Jo Rene for some reason thinks of a county deputy she's seen at the sheriff's office several times the last few months. He's skinny and ugly and reminds her of Barney on "The Andy Griffith Show." The last time she asked him about their investigation into Kari's disappearance, he shrugged and said, "You ever seen that movie *Close Encounters of the Third Kind*?"

THE WEARY MOTEL

Seventeen

Before she leaves Manchester, Jo Rene drives down River Avenue to see how many of the chain letters have been found. Three or four of the cars she put them on are gone. A fat woman with only wisps of orange hair, her head mostly bald, is removing one of the letters from the windshield of a Pinto. Jo Rene slows down. The woman glares at the letter for a couple of seconds, then crumples it, and tosses it over the flood wall.

Winding her way home on the narrow road to Peebles, Jo Rene turns the radio up loud, trying to blast everything out of her head, especially thoughts of the Barbie doll. The sun is setting fast. The landscape is gray—quickly vanishing. She thinks about stupid things: Does Dolly Parton's back hurt? Did Michael Jackson change the color of his eyes? Did Elvis really like to have sex with dead people?

The news comes on.

Heather Burns, Pumpkin Festival Queen of Adams County, is still missing. Authorities are interviewing friends and relatives.

A woman in Maryland was in court today because she traded her infant son for a Camaro Z-28 sports car. She told the judge she thought it was a good idea at first, but when she found out what her auto insurance would be, she wanted her baby back.

Jo Rene thinks about how in high school she swore she never wanted kids because most kids just made their parents

miserable. If she had a daughter, she might grow up to be a drug
addict or a prostitute or worse. Jo Rene would never be able to
control her and would have to spend all her money bailing the kid
out of jail, and still, the daughter would say, "I hate you. I hate
you." A son would be worse.

Then she had Kari and worried not about her own life
being ruined but only about Kari's life being a disaster. Jo Rene
was certain that whatever Kari became she would be the product
of the home provided for her, not just the amount of pain the world
inflicted on her.

Jo Rene changes the radio station, thinking about Burt
Reynolds being bald, about Chevy Chase being bald, about Bruce
Willis being bald, about Elvis being bald.

Elvis. She hopes Scott goes bald. He's so arrogant, thinks
he's God's gift. Bald and fat with rotten teeth—that's how she'd
like to see him. She hopes he dies lonely.

The first week she lived with him she thought she had
found Heaven. He made love to her a couple of hours every night
and came home from the car lot for forty-five minutes during his
lunch break if she wasn't working at Kentucky Fried Chicken.
She didn't care that his apartment was full of roaches and dust
balls and that there wasn't a single decoration on the walls. She'd
bring home chicken for supper, or she'd make grilled-cheese
sandwiches. Scott drank a few beers. Some nights he went to bars
to perform, and she went with him, proud watching him tell jokes
or sing, annoyed that the crowds never paid much attention to him
and made a lot of noise.

Then Scott lost his day job. She came home one evening
from work and he was already there. He still had on the required
outfit for Manchester Motors: dark slacks, a white shirt, a navy
blue tie. The owner of the business insisted that consumers
trusted only conservatively dressed salesmen, that they wouldn't
buy a used car from flashy guys or hippies. Scott once said, "If I
had a bicycle, everyone would think I was a Jehovah's Witness."

Scott was on the brown sofa with a beer in his hand,
watching cartoons, "Looney Toons." He had loosened his tie and
taken off his black wing-tips. Jo Rene liked the way he was
sprawled on the sofa, the way his pants fit him. She knew something was wrong, but she almost couldn't care—she had turned

into a sex maniac, and nothing else in life seemed as important. She had thought that only guys could be obsessed with sex, but Scott had done something to her, had changed her; something—or maybe everything—about him tugged powerfully at her heart and her body.

"Why you home early, honey?" she said and touched his soft hair.

"Old man Gosgrove fired me," he said casually.

"Fired you?" She bent down and studied his face to make sure he wasn't joking. "He can't do that."

"He can't?" Scott looked at her as if maybe she knew about some law he wasn't aware of. "Why can't he?"

"I . . . I don't know. He just can't."

"Shit." His face turned red. A thick vein suddenly bulged from his forehead. "You don't know fuck."

"I know I love you and we'll be okay." She sat down next to him and tried to hug him.

"Get the fuck off. Shit. You know what he said? He said I was too pushy." Scott was sitting up on the edge of the sofa now.

"You're not pushy."

"I know I'm not." He crushed his beer can. "Fuck him."

"That's right."

"Some guy, some customer—well, not really a customer, the son of bitch didn't even buy a car—said I was pushy."

"The guy went to Gosgrove and told him that?"

"Not exactly. You know how Cosgrove calls every asshole that comes on the lot? Jesus, if somebody just stopped by to take a piss in the john, Cosgrove'd have them sign the visitors' book. So he calls this guy and asks him how his visit to the lot was. You know, kissin' the guy's ass to try to get him to come back and buy a car, and the guy told him I was too pushy. Cosgrove said other people have said the same thing. He said I get up in people's faces and I act nervous and sweat. I don't sweat. I'm a fuckin' professional performer. Sweat. Shit. You ever hear such a screwy fuckin' thing? Get fired because you sweat. I guess *he* doesn't sweat in the middle of summer."

She tried to hug him again, but he said, "Get the fuck out of my face."

*

At home, the house is dark. Not even the porch light is on. Jo Rene wonders where Buck could be as she fumbles blindly with the lock on the front door.

Inside, she turns on the lights. She calls Buck's name just in case. Maybe he went to bed sick. But he's not upstairs in their bedroom.

He has been here, though. The closet he keeps his things in is open—and empty.

Eighteen

Dill waits in his truck in front of The Sweet Time Dairy Bar in Manchester for Lori to show up. About a hundred yards away, the Ohio River flows by high and muddy. The Sweet Time stays open all year, and even on cold, damp nights like tonight, customers stop by for ice-cream cones and sundaes. The McDonald's down the street sells yogurt now instead of ice-cream, but The Sweet Time still sells the stuff that will rot your teeth and clog your arteries.

Lori gives her patients little booklets that tell them to avoid anything that tastes good—at least that's how Dill sees it. He has always been suspicious of dentists trying to make people feel guilty for eating sugar and for not brushing and flossing ten times a day. When he's kidded her about being a rich dentist, Lori has insisted that dentistry isn't as good a career as it was in the old days before fluoride was put in everybody's drinking water. Her saying that supports his belief that dentists are secretly glad their warnings are ignored by most people. Dentists love cavities and gum diseases—money in the bank. A dentist one time told Dad that Jo Rene needed ten fillings. Dad took her to another dentist who said she needed three.

You can't trust anybody, Dill believes. He winces thinking about what Lori did to him two years ago, putting him to sleep and drilling holes through four of his teeth. He guesses she could have done worse. He squeezes his knees together while he looks

at The Sweet Time, a small hut (green like a bad tooth) with
windows covered with last summer's fly specks. Lori drilled those
holes because, she said, she loved him so much.

Dill hasn't seen her since the night before Thanksgiving.
When they talked on the phone yesterday, she said she had to tell
him something. Her voice sounded sad. It had a catch in it when
she told him she loved him. Of the things that can be wrong, Dill
has focused on the possibility that she has breast cancer. There's
always something on TV about it, and Lori's thirty-six and has big
breasts. He has heard that flat-chested women don't have to worry
so much.

Six years ago, the woman who "kidnapped" him one
weekend and took him to Tennessee, died of breast cancer. Vicki.
She had big breasts, like Lori. He feels creepy knowing that he
squeezed Vicki's breasts after they were already full of cancer, and
he feels guilty that he didn't notice the lumps—she could have
gone to the doctor sooner, and Dill could have felt good about
saving her life. He thinks hard about the weight and contours of
Lori's breasts.

Last night he had trouble sleeping. He lay stretched on
his back, his throat dry, and thought about making love to Lori.

And he kept thinking about breast cancer.

Two years ago, Dill lost a lot of sleep. He wanted Lori to
leave her husband, but she wouldn't because they had the dental
practice together and because of her little girls. She also didn't
want to risk losing her house, a restored 1817 stone mansion. Dill
figured she mainly didn't want to hook up permanently with a
loser like him.

Lori's kids are eight and ten now. During that bad time
two years ago, Dill got his first glimpse of them. He was driving
down the Appalachian Highway one Sunday morning when Lori's
Caprice Classic suddenly came up behind him and then passed
him in the outside lane. Her husband was driving, and her kids
were in the back seat. The four of them were dressed up. Lori
stared straight ahead, ignoring Dill.

He pressed the truck's accelerator to come up beside them
again to get another look. Her husband was pale and thin and had
orange hair and an orange beard. No wonder Lori wanted a lover,
Dill thought. The little girls had orange hair and big splotches of

freckles—ugly kids. The Caprice pulled ahead again. Dill drove faster to catch up. The little girls were staring at him. Lori's husband was saying something to Lori, probably about the asshole in the pickup truck. Lori just stared straight ahead. Dill wanted her to look at him, to acknowledge him in some way. He didn't like being ignored as if he didn't count, didn't exist. His face felt hot, and he pumped the accelerator so that the truck roared. Then he noticed a dog, a cocker spaniel, in the back seat with the little girls. She'd never told him they had a dog. That made him even madder for some reason.

When the Caprice slowed down, he slowed down. Lori's husband honked at him, and Dill honked back and flipped him the bird. Suddenly, the Caprice cut into a left-hand turn lane, and looking back, Dill saw it pull into the lot of a Methodist church.

The next time he and Lori saw each other, she threw a phone book at him. He ducked and it smashed against the wall of their motel room. She shouted that he was stupid, crazy, dangerous. She said her husband asked her whether she knew him. She cried.

Dill wanted to know why she never told him about the dog. He wanted to know what the fuck the dog did at church.

She slapped him, and he slapped her back. She bit him. He pinched her. They took all their clothes off, and she had five orgasms. Finally, they just held each other. She admitted that she liked the way he cared so much.

He usually got to see Lori only once a week. Often, around eleven at night while he and Dawnell watched MTV, Dill would suddenly be hit by a vision of Lori in bed with her husband. Most of the sexy women in the videos on MTV reminded him of Lori.

One Friday night when he was feeling miserable, thinking about Lori being at a dentists convention in New Orleans, he went to the Love's Quick Stop and talked the check-out girl, Tonya, into going on a camping trip with him that weekend. She was bone-thin and always looked sleepy and moved lazily.

Dill's and the girl's shadows were big on the wall of their tent dimly lit by an electric lantern. The shadows were the next best thing to having a mirror. Dill liked the narrowness of the girl's waist and hips and her thin thighs, but while he was on her, she kept her head turned to one side and seemed distracted. When he looked around, he saw that she had her hands above his back and was making shadow animals.

Nineteen

*L*ori finally shows up at The Sweet Time, but she doesn't park. She pulls into the lot, turns around, and Dill follows her Caprice Classic to Water Street. There's a nice restaurant on this street called The River View, but they've never eaten there because Lori is afraid of being recognized. Dentists are famous. In fact, Lori and her husband recently started running an ad in the Adams County paper each week with their pictures: The Harrison Family Dental Clinic. The picture is in black and white, so you can't tell that Lori's husband has orange hair. A good thing, Dill thinks.

A lot of people were saying hi to Lori the first time Dill saw her. He was grocery shopping at the Kroger supermarket in Peebles. He had picked up six or seven women over the years in grocery stores. Often they came on to him first, asking something like whether he knew where the hot sauce was or the spices or what kind of light bulbs burned the longest. He noticed Lori giving him the eye by the frozen-food section. She was wearing a fur coat and a fat diamond ring, a diamond wrist watch, a diamond necklace, and diamond earrings. He asked her whether those Lean Cuisine frozen dinners were really as good as people claimed and worth the money. She told him it was obvious to her that he needed some professional oral care, that he should make an appointment for a Wednesday. She gave him her business card.

Her husband never worked on Wednesdays. She told Dill

that Harry usually drove to Cincinnati to visit buddies from dental school or to do some kind of vague research at the university library and that he never got back home until well after midnight. Lori was almost certain he had a girl there, probably some young thing with an overbite–Harry thought overbites were very sexy. All the girls working at the Harrison Family Dental Clinic—three dental assistants and the receptionist—had overbites.

The first time Lori and Dill went to a motel, she said, "You know, I think that instead of me wearing black panties or something, Harry would rather have me put on some fake buck teeth."

The time she drilled the holes in Dill's teeth they met at her office late at night. He was worried because she said he almost definitely had mouth cancer. He didn't even fantasize about making love to her in one of the dental chairs.

He still doesn't know how she found out about the camping trip. It's disturbing to think she has mysterious ways of finding things out about him. He wonders whether it's true the FBI has a file on everybody. If so, he wonders what it says about him. "Stud"? Probably, "loser," "lousy father."

In his early teens, he did some shop lifting and smoked joints on the bank of the river. He stole a car one time, a junky Chrysler, which threw a rod in Brown County. He had to walk home at three in the morning. He was afraid to hitch hike. He was terrified that some psycho would pick him up and sacrifice him to Satan or something, so when cars came past, he crouched down in the ditch or in some weeds.

When he was fourteen, he drank a lot of cheap wine.

He spied on a divorced woman who sometimes left her window shades half way up while she undressed.

And he used to follow his daddy, used to spy through the windows of restaurants and bars and the Manchester Bowl-o-rama on Daddy and his crippled women. Daddy had a thing for women with handicaps.

On an empty street in Manchester one Sunday evening just at dusk, Dill tried to rob an old blind man. He walked up to the man, who had a cane but no dark glasses, his eyes roaming around out of control, gross and useless. Dill had just seen Daddy lean across a table in Wanda's Family Restaurant and kiss the lips of a one-armed woman.

Dill said to the blind man, "Stop." He shoved his hand against the man's chest and was surprised that the chest was hard. "I got . . . got a gun . . . motherfucker. Give me your money."

The blind man shook his head slowly, his tongue flicking out to wet his lips.

"Come on. The money."

The man kept shaking his head.

"You deaf, too, you blind bastard?"

Dill started shivering. He heard footsteps, heels clicking on the sidewalk. He turned his head. Then the blind man's cane cracked against the side of his head, and Dill went down. He wasn't sure how long he was down but not long. He got up, stumbled, ran. He had never run so hard in his life, his sneakers slapping the sidewalk loudly. He was scared of what he had done, of getting caught, and of what he was becoming. The side of his head throbbed. His vision was blurred. When he got home, he hid in his room for three days.

Carol saved him. Her love gave him a purpose and a focus. She eased all the pains. Otherwise, he might have ended up in prison or dead. Then Dawnell was his purpose. He couldn't get too wild with a child to care for. Now Lori, too. He loves Lori the way he loved Carol sixteen years ago.

Carol, Dawnell, Lori. The most important people in his life.

Lori parks along the flood wall. When she gets in the truck, they kiss. She tastes like peppermint.

"I thought I saw one of my patients back there at the dairy bar. That's why I didn't stop."

"That's okay. I was just startin' to worry about where you were."

"I would have met you on time, but I was trying to convince Harry that I really was going to visit my sister."

"What if he calls her to see if you're there?"

"She's out of town. If he calls there, I'll say we decided to go to a movie."

"What movie?"

"I don't know. I'll tell him it was a porno movie." She grins at Dill.

"What's it that you need to tell me? You sick?"

"We'll talk later," she says.

"No. I wanta know. You sick?"

"Let's just have a good time now."

"Are you sick?"

"No. I'm not sick."

"You sure?"

"Yes, I'm sure. I'm not sick."

They can see the lights of tug boats as they drive along the river and lights on the Kentucky side. Dill is suddenly giddy with lust. They smile at each other every few seconds, and Dill squeezes her thigh. Lori is wearing a broach, a necklace, rings on every finger, a studded belt. Diamonds, rubies, sapphires. More diamonds. She sparkles all over.

Dill has accepted seeing Lori only four or five times a month, accepted the fact that money and children bind her to a man with orange hair. His acceptance has been gradual. It's like a handicap he's learned to live with that causes only occasional pain.

They drive through Aberdeen, and when they come to the bridge, they see a banner hanging down from a couple of the cross beams that says, "WE LOVE YOU HEATHER."

"I hope that girl's not really in this river," Dill says.

"She was pretty," Lori says.

They cross the bridge into Maysville—a sign says, "Home of Rosemary Clooney"—then wind up a mountain, on top of which is their favorite motel. It's a bright vision in the night. The El Rancho. Flood lights illuminate giant blue steers and golden bulls and white horses all made of plaster and spray painted with high-gloss enamel. And there are other animals, ones you don't find on a ranch. A purple zebra. A pink giraffe. They all graze in the parking lot.

Twenty

Dill grazes between Lori's thighs. Her noises wash over him. His skin tingles. He moves up onto her, and his vision seems peculiarly sharp. The oranges and browns and yellows of the room glow. Lori is radiant beneath him. She likes the lights on. She says Dill is a gorgeous man.

"Rinnnngggggggggggg!" she shouts. Like a telephone. She says her ears ring when she has an orgasm. "Rinnnngggggggggg!" She's letting him know that he's doing a good job, that she appreciates him, that she loves him.

Afterward, he lies on her and kisses her eyelids. He touches her face with just the tips of his fingers. He bites her shoulder, licks her neck. But then she pats his back frantically and says, "Oh, darling, I'm getting a cramp in my leg. You need to—"

When he rolls off her, he gets a strong whiff of stale cigarettes from the bolted-down ashtray on the night stand. Dill makes a mental note never to bolt down ashtrays in his motel. Lori is smiling at him.

He says, "I love you more than I do my truck."

"Your truck is a pile of junk."

"Yeah, but I love it. It's the one thing I don't owe money on."

Lori doesn't say anything for a moment. She seems to study his face. "You're good to me."

"I gotta be. You're a scary woman. You and your dentist drills."

"Do you have to bring that up all the time? I was insane. I've grown up a lot since then."

"You mean I can see other women and you won't come after me with a drill? Lady dentist from Hell." He pretends his finger is a drill and forces her mouth open.

She kisses his finger, then says, "I was so jealous then. It was stupid."

"I forgive you." He pretends his finger is a drill again, and she sucks it. "Your leg still crampin'?"

"No."

He kisses her, decides to try to make her ring again.

*

A cold drizzle is falling when they leave the El Rancho. The giant animals in the parking lot seem to Dill like reminders of the dangers of the world they're returning to. The pale-pink giraffe makes him think of Lori's husband.

The vinyl seat of the truck is cold. Lori looks older than she did a few minutes ago, but she still looks good. She has confessed to him that she used to drink a lot. Chugged vodka when she was fifteen. Now she goes to AA meetings, has for five years. Dill thought booze always ruined a person's looks. He remembers the way Daddy looked the last few months he was alive, the broken vessels in his nose, his slack jowls, the sloppy belly. He thinks that one day all of Lori's past abuse may go off under her skin like a time bomb. As much as he likes her looks, he's pretty certain he'll still love her after her looks are gone. If Carol were alive and had gotten really fat or something, he'd still love *her*. He has a philosophy. Some women need to keep their looks to keep their men, but if real love is involved, the looks shouldn't matter so much. He has seen old men pinch their wives' big saggy butts, and it makes him smile, makes him happy, makes him think the world's not all bad.

Dill drives down the mountain into Maysville slowly. Fog has swallowed up the town. The Ohio River has vanished. Dill's truck creeps through the streets. As they approach the bridge, Lori says, "I need to tell you something."

He forgot he was worried about her. "You're pregnant," he says, half kidding, half hoping.

"No."

"Then you must want to borrow money."

"I was going to tell you back in the room, but . . . ."

The bridge makes a high whine as they cross it. Dill sees the back of the banner hanging down, can't see the words. The truck feels unsteady, wobbles. On the Ohio side there's a patch of bright street lights, and Lori's jewels sparkle. Then there are no lights, and Dill can barely see her beside him. He starts to worry again—worry hard.

Breast cancer. He squints, trying to see through the fog.

"What is it?" he says.

"I've been seeing somebody else."

For a minute, Dill forgets to breath. "A man?"

"I've been seeing him for ten weeks."

"That's impossible."

"No."

"But . . . . How? I mean, how can you see me and somebody else, too?"

"I've been forced to lie to Harry a lot lately. I've missed some work."

"I didn't mean how do you find the time." Suddenly, he wants to hit her. "I meant another kind of how." He swallows, and his throat hurts. His lips feel bruised.

"It really has been awful."

"I bet it has."

"You don't have to be nasty. He's a nice man. He's a lawyer—"

"What's his name?"

"You don't know him."

"What's his name?"

"It's not important."

"I just wanta know his name."

"Bruce."

"Bruce," Dill says softly. He hates her. She's a broken-down alcoholic who whores around.

"I didn't plan anything to happen. He's married, too."

"I thought only fags were named Bruce."

"He's going to tell his wife about us, and I think I'm finally going to make a break from Harry."

Dill looks at her, his mouth open.

"Watch the road, please," she says.

"You'll leave your husband for this guy? What about your fucking dental practice? What about your fucking kids? Huh? What about your fucking *house*?"

"Dill, honey, I'll always love you. But I love Bruce, too. And I have to be practical."

A long time ago, she told him about a real-estate agent she had had an affair with before her daughters were born. He wonders now how many men she hasn't mentioned. Once when they were making love, she said nobody had ever made love to her the way he did. *Nobody.* The way she said it implied large numbers. He thinks she told him about the real-estate agent because she thought he'd laugh at her story of how the guy could talk just like Donald Duck, how sometimes he did his Donald Duck impersonation while they were in bed. She's crying now, but Dill doesn't care. He considers slamming the truck into a tree.

"I'm going to miss you," she says.

"You're the craziest bitch I ever met."

"Fine, Dill. Be a child."

"Jesus. You loved me so much you nearly killed me two years ago. What happened to that love?"

"I'm a complex person."

"You're a crazy bitch."

The fog continues to be thick along the road to Manchester. Red and blue and yellow lights appear suddenly, and he pulls over. The lights are neon beer signs in the windows of a run-down tavern. He pulls into a parking slot between two cars. A Miller High Life sign blinks a couple of feet from the hood of the truck. The cab is filled with shadows and colors coming and going. Lori is there one moment, her face red, blue, yellow—then she's gone, swallowed up in the blackness.

She says, "Tell me you still love me. It would make me feel a lot better."

Dill glares at her. He wants to beat the shit out of her. He wants to beg her not to do this to him. Faint music comes from the tavern. A whiny hillbilly sound.

Twenty-one

In the middle of the night Jo Rene wakes up freezing and sick to her stomach. She lies shivering and hovers somewhere on the edge of sleep. A strobe light turns in her head, casting streaks of lurid colors onto the black back drop of her eye lids. Then the real show starts: the Barbie doll from the flea market comes to life inside its box, only to turn purple suddenly—to suffocate behind its cellophane.

Later, after she has kneeled before the toilet, the tile floor like ice to her feet and knees, she dreams of her father and Buck and Scott and Kari all riding in her father's '57 Plymouth down a straight, wide highway in a desert where the cactus multiply with each revolution of the car's wheels until the desert becomes a forest of cactus, then a forest of pine trees. Now Elvis Presley is driving the car, a fat bald man in a silver jump suit, and Jo Rene's father, Kari, and Scott are all in the back seat, and the road is suddenly full of bumps that make Elvis' wide lapels flap up and down and hair-pin curves that cause Kari to scream gleefully. Then Jo Rene is in her mother's kitchen, trying to read a chain letter, but the words are blurred. Buck is there, talking, but his voice is muffled. The kitchen is cold, cold. It begins to snow outside. Her dog Rex bites Buck's good hand off, and Buck screams for help. Blood spews from his stump. Earthquake. An earthquake makes the floor boards roll like ocean waves.

A shrill ringing pulls her up out of her delirious sleep, her hellish half death. The ringing hurts her ears, and she thinks of Buck telling her she shouldn't play her car radio so loud; he told her about warnings on MTV that loud noises or music could cause hearing loss.

Finally, she knows what's ringing. She reaches blindly toward the night stand and turns off the alarm clock, and in the cold, still silence, she realizes that she's already thinking of Buck in the past tense.

*

During the night she thought she might die, but she's already feeling better—physically, at least—and the heartache of Buck's leaving takes over, pressing her into the mattress of her bed, darkening the edges of her vision when she dares to open her eyes to the ceiling crisscrossed by thin cracks.

She remembers being nine years old and Mom lying in the dark with her hair dirty and her face gaunt, Mom crying softly, a rough wool blanket pulled up close under her chin, Jo Rene deciding it was up to herself to hold the world together and saying, "You have to eat, Mom."

Jo Rene dragged a chair over to the kitchen counter to get the tomato soup down from the cabinet, then scooted the chair over to the stove. The flames of the burner appeared in a small explosion, leaping yellow then steady blue. Pretty.

Mom wouldn't eat anything except a cracker, the tray balancing on her knees unsteadily. Jo Rene made tea, too, and Mom took one sip.

"Get your brother," Mom said. "I want to talk to him. For just a second. Tell him it's just for a second. Tell him I'm not going to yell at him."

"Dill's not here." Dill was fourteen. Since Dad had left, Dill had been out somewhere all the time, except for a few hours each night when he slept in his locked room.

"Tell him I want to see him when he comes home."

"Okay. Eat your soup."

Mom didn't, though. She didn't even look at it. The tray wiggled on her knees. Her nose was red, redder than her lips without their lipstick.

"You want me to make you up?" Jo Rene asked. But Mom shook her head, slowly.

Sometimes she let Jo Rene brush her hair and put make-up on her. "Daddy will think you oughta be on TV," Jo Rene would say. And Mom would laugh, looking like a clown, kind of, because Jo Rene always smeared the lipstick on thick and beyond Mom's lips. Mom's lips needed to be fuller.

This was the third time Daddy had deserted them. Each time, he left because of a woman. And each woman was crippled.

The first time, Mom had not lain around sad. She stuffed his shirts, pants, socks, belts, underwear, and handyman books into paper grocery sacks she saved under the kitchen sink. (Daddy was always saying the bags attracted roaches.) Mom made Jo Rene and Dill help her put the sacks by the street for the garbage collectors. Dill was only twelve then and still did things she told him to do.

Mom stood for a long time at the front window, looking at the pile of overflowing paper bags at the edge of the front yard. She said, "That bastard is crazy," and shook her head.

The garbage men weren't due to come for three days. Jo Rene noticed that people stopped on the sidewalk and pointed at the house. Some of them laughed. That night, it rained and dogs ripped open the bags. In the morning Daddy's clothes and handy-man books were strewn all over the yard and street. Pages from the books blew into the neighbors' yards. Daddy liked to fix things. He bragged that he could fix *anything*. Wiring, plumbing, cracked foundations. "You name it," he said, and his hand holding his cigarette would shake as he raised it to his lips.

As the days passed, Mom continued to stare out the window. When she wasn't doing that, she watched TV, throwing potato chips or bread crusts or pieces of cheese rolled into little balls at the screen. Some of the cheese stuck to the people on the TV, to the handsome men and the goofy men and to the beautiful women with the full lips who were getting kissed all the time.

The first time Mom threw food at the TV, Dill and Jo Rene laughed, but Mom yelled, "What are you laughing at? You little turds. You bugs. You shits. You brats." She glared at them, her small breasts (one drooping lower than the other) heaving. "He probably couldn't stand being around you little turds anymore.

And you better not tell anybody he ran off with a woman." Jo Rene turned her head toward the living-room window and looked at the clothes and books and wet, torn paper bags in the yard and street. "It's nobody's business. I'll beat the crap out of both of you. I swear it. If anybody asks where he is, tell them he's on a business trip. A bakers' convention." Mom's eyes shifted away, darted around, fixed on the *TV Guide*. "In Las Vegas." Then her eyes widened, slid up the wall behind the television and studied a picture of Jesus leading sheep. "No. Tulsa. Tell them he went to Tulsa. For a bakers' convention."

Daddy made donuts for a living. He would bring home donuts every day.

"Your soup's getting cold," Jo Rene said, but Mom just lay in her bed, staring at the pile of her and Daddy's dirty clothes in a dark corner. With the curtains closed and the only light coming through the door from the hall, Jo Rene could barely see the dirty clothes, but she could smell them—sweat and perfume and Daddy's sweet cologne. She could smell the tomato soup, too.

"I'm gonna kill myself," Mom said.

"The soup is Campbell's soup."

Mom didn't say anything for a while. Jo Rene watched Mom's hand, waiting for it to rise and take the spoon and dip it into the soup. The tray trembled, and some of the soup spilled. "You and your brother can go live with your grandmother."

"You want some cheese for your crackers?"

Mom closed her eyes and lay still. After a while, her lips parted slightly with a soft pop.

Jo Rene went to the kitchen and made herself a cheese sandwich, and she chewed it and chewed it, but she couldn't swallow. It just wouldn't go down her throat. Finally, she spit it out. She thought about taking money from her mother's purse and going to the grocery store to get some donuts.

The first woman Daddy left them for worked in the bakery with him. She was confined to a wheel chair and sat all day at a low table, kneading and twisting dough. One Saturday not long before he went to live with her, he took Jo Rene with him to work. The woman didn't try to make conversation with Jo Rene. She stayed focused on the dough in front of her, her hands working hard. She was not pretty. She needed to wear make-up. Her legs were skinny like the spokes of the wheels of her chair. Her white socks drooped. In the car on the way home, Daddy said she was born with a twisted spine. He shook his head and looked sad.

He lived with this woman for about a month. The night he returned home, he came into Jo Rene's room and kissed her forehead, and she woke up. He was tall and lean. His shoulders sagged. He always kept his big hands in his pockets.

"I'm sorry I've been gone," he said. He seemed to be looking at the small bookcase in the corner. "No one ever loved her before. She needed me. Do you understand?"

Jo Rene just stared at him.

Then Mom was in the room. "She kicked you out."

"I'll talk to you in a minute. I want to see Dill, too."

"The little crippled bitch told you to get the hell out. I heard it all from her own sister. She didn't want to be your holy mission in life, your personal charity case."

When he left again about a year later, Mom didn't yell like the first time. She sat in the living room without the TV on. She made Dill and Jo Rene fix their own cheese sandwiches. The second woman was someone Jo Rene used to see on her walk to school each day. The woman sat on the sagging porch of an old house, wearing a black sweater (regardless of the weather) covered with lint. Her hair was red and wild, and she didn't have a right arm.

The third woman wore a white eye patch, and half of her face looked like a melted pink candle.

Jo Rene remembers making paper dolls the third time Daddy went away. She remembers the sound of her scissors as she made paper moms and daddies and kids, about forty of them. She colored their faces and hair and clothes. She knew Mom would be mad, but she glued them up all over the house. She put up most of them in her room. And on Dill's locked door. And on Mom's door. The paper dolls had happy faces, and Jo Rene imagined Daddy laughing and liking them when he came home.

She knew he would come home. He just felt sorry for ladies who had something wrong with them. She had come to realize that he thought he could fix them. But he couldn't stay with them long. He always changed his mind about loving them. He tried to fix them, but he just ended up breaking their hearts.

Then he would come home.

Twenty-two

Dill is sitting in his truck in front of The Weary's office. He is no longer a human being. He has become nothing more than a raw nerve. Six feet, one hundred and eighty pounds of pain. In his truck's rearview mirror, before he goes inside the motel's office, he looks at his eyes, red from no sleep, and the dark crescents under them. His face has gone slack. His bones feel soft.

The first thing Dill sees when he stumbles in is the sign on the wall saying "ONLY MISSING." George is sitting behind the desk that divides the office, reading the sports page of the morning paper and shaking his head. "Hell of a thing," he says.

Dill stares at the black velvet pictures of Elvis and James Dean and Jim Morrison. Marilyn Monroe. He's struck by how much Marilyn reminds him of Lori.

George looks up. "Hey. Hey, you're bleedin'."

"What?"

"You're bleedin'. Did you know you're bleedin'?" George nods at the hand Dill has resting on the desk.

In a detached way, Dill turns his attention to the blood oozing from his palm. It's creating a small puddle from which two red rivulets spread.

Earlier this morning he stopped his truck when he saw a cow, a Jersey heifer, sleeping in the fog near the road. He climbed a barbed-wire fence, approached the cow stealthily, then shoved it as hard as he could. When he was a kid, friends told him it was funny as hell to tip over sleeping cows, to watch them fall like cardboard stand-ups, but he never tried it himself. When he shoved the heifer this morning, it didn't budge. Dill slipped and fell on his back. A rock gouged him between his shoulder blades. The cow turned its head and looked down at him. Maybe it wasn't asleep after all.

When he was climbing back over the fence, a section of it collapsed, and that was when he sliced his hand. He ended up on the ground in a tangle of barbed wire.

"You got mud on your butt," George says. "And blood on the front of your pants." George has stood up and come around the desk and is looking Dill over. "Did you win or lose?"

"Huh?"

"The fight."

"It wasn't . . . ." Dill looks out at the parking spaces in front of the rooms. There's not a single car. "No guests at all," Dill whispers.

"We got some Mercurochrome in the first-aid kit." George opens a drawer in the desk and pulls out a white plastic box. He takes Dill's hand and presses a towel to it to stop the bleeding. "Looks to me like you lost."

"What?"

George takes the towel away and examines the wound. Then he gently spreads the medicine. "Hurts like hell, don't it?" George says. And he looks into Dill's eyes. George's eyes are gray and shiny and surrounded by wrinkles. It's a long time before Dill can look away.

*

Dill watches George drive off doing about five miles an hour. George always sits at the blind curve for a long time. He rolls down his window, cocks his ear, sniffs the air, then finally gets up the nerve to creep out into the road, his big old car like a yacht, and putters out of sight, gray smoke hanging above the road for a long time after he's gone.

Dill turns away from the window and goes around behind the desk where he steps in a pile of wood shavings. This is the first time George hasn't cleaned up the mess from his whittling.

Dill doesn't understand whittling. George takes a stick, strips it of its bark, smooths it, sharpens it into a little spear, then whittles it into nothing. Dill has asked George what the purpose is. George says that the purpose is the pleasure his hands and mind get out of it.

Dill's bottom lip trembles. His stomach hurts. He was a little better while George was here, but he couldn't tell George anything, couldn't get the words out, and now George is gone.

"The bitch blew me away," Dill says aloud. "The whore." Jesus, his hand hurts.

Dill sits down in the green, padded swivel chair that always leans to one side or the other, and he stares at nothing for a while before closing his eyes.

He dreams about hospital smells, the ones he remembers from the summer he was an orderly, the summer he was sixteen. He was overwhelmed by the smells of bedpans and puke and cleaning fluids and medicine. The flowers he sometimes delivered to patients' rooms usually smelled too sweet, made his nose tickle, but he'd steal a rose, a tulip, or a daisy and put it in his locker and take it to Carol the next day. In the afternoons when he had to leave her, he would have the smell of her on his right hand. He avoided washing it off, and throughout the night, he would close his eyes and lift his hand to his face and inhale her deeply and ache with missing her.

In his dream, Dill sees yellow, brown, purple, and red clouds of smells hovering in a long hallway of the Adams County General Hospital. He hurries down the hall and through double doors and into a field of mud. Then he's climbing the stairs of a tower in the middle of a corn field, and some guy in a dark three-piece suit on his way down the stairs passes him and says, "Move over." Dill says, "Asshole." The guy in the suit drives away fast in a brown Cadillac. Dawnell is at the top of the tower holding something dark and bloody in her hands. "Is that liver?" Dill says. "You gonna cook it?" She flings it out over the tower wall, and Dill watches the hunk of flesh fall and fall and fall . . . .

"Dill," Jo Rene says.

"What?" Dill says, and then he's awake.

"What the hell happened to you?"

"I was tippin' cows, and one tipped me instead."

"What?"

He rubs his good hand all over his face. "Listen, sis. We had us a zero occupancy rate last night, so you might as well go home."

"No, I'll clean."

"What for? I just told you there weren't any guests last night. You gonna change clean sheets?"

"I'll dust."

"And polish the silver?"

"What?"

"Go home. You look tired. I'll give you some money." Dill reaches into his back pocket for his wallet and discovers it missing. "Oh no."

"What?"

"I think I lost my wallet in that cow pasture." He starts laughing.

"You all right, Dill?"

He keeps laughing. Then he starts trembling all over.

"Dill? What's wrong, Dill? Tell me."

"Nothin'." Dill stops laughing. He sits, his arms dangling between his thighs. He stares at his hands, feels drained.

"No, I mean it, Dill. Tell me."

A raw nerve. He starts shaking his head, slow at first, then faster and faster.

"What are you doing? You're going to scramble your brains."

Then he buries his face in his big hands, and his shoulders tremble, but his eyes stay dry, feel rough as sand paper. He feels Jo Rene's hands patting his shoulders. Finally, he's able to say, "I loved her. I loved her."

"Did Lori dump you?"

Dill nods, the tears pouring.

Jo Rene gets a rickety wooden chair from a corner and sits close to Dill. She takes his hands.

"I hate her," Dill says.

"I know." Jo Rene starts crying.

Dill looks up. "What is it? What's wrong with *you*?"

"Buck left."

"He what?"

"He never came home. I knew it was coming. I don't think I really loved him, though. Not much. Not the way I used to love . . . Scott."

Dill and Jo Rene are quiet for a minute. They don't look at each other.

"I'm sorry," Dill says.

Jo Rene says, "You know, falling out of love can feel as good as falling in love. It's such a relief." She wipes her eyes with the back of her hand.

"You want me to kill Buck for you?"

"You want me to kill Lori for *you*?"

Dill hangs his head again, and snot drips from his nose. "No. I'll do it myself."

The Weary Motel

Twenty-three

It's Sunday evening, and Jo Rene is trying to put together the artificial Christmas tree she bought last January at K-mart for $8.95, marked down from $19.95. A smart buy, she thought. Real trees shed needles all over the place and are fire hazards. Every Christmas morning there's a news story about a family burning up.

Buck promised to help with the tree, but she should have known better than to put stock in a man's promise. She's determined not to think about Buck, but she can't help thinking about how she has never had a man around at Christmas time.

The phone rings, and at first it sounds like an obscene call, somebody trying to disguise his voice. Then she realizes it's Dill. Jo Rene can't make out what he's saying. His voice is loud and distorted. Jo Rene can tell by the slur of his words that he's drunk.

"Slow down, Dill. You're mumbling like a retarded person. Calm down. Is it something about Lori?"

"Naw. Naw."

"Is somebody dead?"

The Christmas-tree lights blur into one another, and Jo Rene rubs at tears, suddenly feels as though her knees will buckle. Maybe Grandma's dead. Maybe that's what Dill's saying. Old people can go in the snap of two fingers. Jo Rene steps closer to the tree—the cheap thing does a poor imitation of a real tree; it's tidier, but you can tell it's plastic, a cold dead thing that never lived. She looks out the window into the dark at the outlines of things that once lived and are now dead: the brown yard, the black trees, the slat gray sky like a blanket God is trying to smother her with.

The sky is the color of the 1957 Plymouth Daddy brought home and painted. It was sky gray, with slanted double headlights that made Jo Rene think of Chinese people's eyes; there were dents and rust spots all over; foam rubber belched out of the seats.

Daddy painted it a color he called sky blue. He didn't put tape on the chrome or windows or remove the rust. He used a paint brush you'd whitewash a fence with.

He had lost his job at the bakery a couple of months before, while he was living with his third crippled woman. He had missed a lot of work to spend time with her. Mom got a job as a hairdresser, which was the job she had had before she got married.

Jo Rene would come home from school and find Daddy drinking beer at the Formica kitchen table and drawing pictures of castles. He said he was designing a castle he planned to build. His drawings were done on Big Chief tablets. Jo Rene told him she liked the drawings.

When he wasn't drawing castles, he spent a lot of time staring at Jo Rene's fish bowl. Then for lunch one day, he fried Jo Rene's three goldfish.

He wouldn't see a doctor, Mom told Jo Rene years later. Mom didn't press him. She was worried about what the doctor's bills would be, and her friends at the beauty salon said she probably needn't worry so much, that men always acted crazy when they were out of work. The friends were praying for him. They told stories about their own husbands or about their fathers or sons or brothers.

When Dad bought the Plymouth with money from the family's small savings, Mom told Jo Rene he was getting well. He needed the car so that he could look for a job, since she took the Buick to the beauty salon. Jo Rene thought the Plymouth was just an old junker, but Mom looked at it as if it were a new Cadillac.

Jo Rene sat in the grass at the side of the house and watched her father slap paint on the roof, then the hood and trunk, then on the doors and fenders. He said, "When you paint, always start at the top and work down. Any professional painter will tell you that."

When he finished, he stood back and studied the job. Paint had run everywhere; it covered most of the chrome and windows. He had paint all over himself.

Jo Rene said, "Blue's really pretty. It's like the fire on the stove."

He just stared, as if in a trance. When Mom came home, she pretended everything was okay. She made no comment about the car and told Jo Rene to get ready for supper. Dill wasn't around. Dill was never around. Jo Rene went inside and washed her hands and ate half of a cheese sandwich and a spoonful of pork and beans, then went to the window to watch her father. He stood in the driveway, the sun setting behind him, his brow furrowed, and his sleeveless undershirt, his brown dress pants, his black shoes all covered with bright blue paint. After the sun set, he became invisible, a ghost, swallowed by the darkness. Jo Rene heard Mom on the phone: "You don't think I should call an ambulance, do you, Louise?" Louise was a friend at the beauty salon. Mom's voice broke. She was silent for a long time. "Okay, okay. I will. Yes. I feel better. I'll just let him be and see . . . ."

In the morning he was gone. Then a week later, Mom appeared in the doorway of Jo Rene's classroom. The teacher went out into the hall, and she and Mom whispered to each other briefly. Everything was strange, eerie—Mom there at school, leaving school when everyone else was staying, the Buick out at the curb. It was about eleven in the morning, and the streets were almost empty. The mailman was walking up to the house as she and Mom pulled into the driveway. He waited as Mom got out of the car, then handed her a wad of junk mail and nodded.

Dill was slouched on the sofa, wearing jeans and a red tee-shirt, peach fuzz on his chin and upper lip, his mouth slack and defiant. A game show was on TV, loud, the contestants hysterical. Mom flicked it off and told Jo Rene to sit down next to her brother. Mom's head was angled down; she seemed to be looking at the blank television screen as she spoke. "Listen, you two. Your father is dead. Think about that for a minute, then get up and go put on a shirt with a collar, Dill. Put on a dress, Jo Rene. Company's comin'."

The next day, the Baptist church was full of flowers,

neighbors, and relatives (mostly cousins and aunts and uncles from Kentucky), and some people Jo Rene had never seen before, but she saw none of the crippled women. The hard, slick pew hurt her behind, and as the preacher talked about valleys and shadows, she stared at the closed casket. *My daddy is in that box? That box is my daddy?*

The Plymouth stayed in the driveway for nearly a year. Jo Rene thought Mom kept the car because Daddy was coming back. The red-headed boy next door, who had come to the funeral and smacked gum during the preacher's eulogy, said her old man was probably just in a nut house—that was why no one got to see the body. Then one day when Jo Rene got home from school, the car was gone. She asked Mom if Daddy was back.

"Good lord, what the hell are you talkin' about?"

"Daddy's car's gone."

"I finally found somebody who'd give me ten dollars and haul it away. Lord, have mercy. Where you get these crazy notions?"

Out on the driveway there were splotches of blue paint where the Plymouth had sat.

Even now, after all these years, Jo Rene has trouble believing her father is dead. Mom has always been vague about his death. Somewhere in Cincinnati. Fell off a bridge? Jumped off a bridge? Pushed off a bridge?

Jo Rene stares out the window, still half expecting him to come down her driveway one of these days in his old Plymouth the color of the sky.

* * *

*

On the other end of the phone line, Dill continues to be hysterical and drunk. Jo Rene is bawling out of control now but then makes out the word "baby."

"What?" she says.

"Dawnell's . . . gonna . . . baby."

"Dawnell's pregnant?"

"Yeah! Yeah! My baby . . . havin' . . . baby!"

Jo Rene grins. "Jesus, that's weird." She wonders who in the world would want to knock up Dawnell. "Is Grandma okay?"

"Grandma?"

"Never mind. So what are you going to do?"

Dill hiccups. "There's . . . gonna . . . be . . . weddin'."

"Really?"

THE WEARY MOTEL

Twenty-four

It's Monday, and the temperature is dropping. The West Union radio station, WRAC, predicted this morning that it will get down close to zero tonight. The weather doesn't usually get this cold until after Christmas, and Tonya hasn't even gotten to quit her job yet—but at the moment she can handle it.

She has the day off, and she's lying on her and Buck's bed, smoking a joint—good home-grown Adams County marijuana, some of the stuff missed last August by the National Guard's helicopter. The state's marijuana eradication program focused on Adams County for two weeks last summer. The sheriff, his deputies, and the National Guard found what they could, harvested it, and burned it. But Tonya wasn't too worried. She knew there were probably as many Mary Jane plants in the county as corn stalks. Man, she just wanted to find one of those bonfires and let the yellow cloud carry her away.

She has on sweat pants and one of Buck's shirts, soft flannel, the elbows worn through. Buck has been really sweet to her. Every day he brings her chocolate cakes or candy (she's addicted to chocolate, she admits), and twice in the past week, he's had red roses delivered to the house. She likes hearing about the funny old people on his mail route, and he's pretty good in bed, eager and grateful—says he hasn't gotten much in months, the poor thing. A couple of times this weekend, she actually had the thought that maybe she won't bolt for Florida in the spring, that she'll stay with Buck and try to be happy, but she has quickly come to her senses. After all, it's too soon to decide anything like that, and going to Florida is her big dream. She shouldn't let some guy get in the way of it, she argues with herself.

She stretches, yawns, feels mellow. The furnace pumps hot air out of the vents nonstop. Tonya likes it hot. Jesus, she doesn't know why she didn't run away to Florida years ago.

Sometimes travelers who come into Love's will say something like, "Gosh, it's beautiful country around here. All the hills and trees."

Tonya says, "It is?" Flat and hot would suit her fine.

She has moved the TV into the bedroom so that she can be comfortable while she watches the soaps and afternoon reruns of "Gilligan's Island," which always cracks her up, and "The Love Boat," which is on now. The people on the love boat are smiling and waving to people on shore, and she thinks about the Highland Ridge Road overpass.

When she was a kid, she would ride her bicycle five miles to that overpass. It ran above State Route 125, and she would lean on the guardrail and wave at all the cars and trucks approaching below. Some people, mostly truckers, waved back. It felt good to wave at cars and trucks; it felt wonderful when people waved back.

For years, she went there and stood and waved for hours. After her parents got divorced when she was nine, she went there almost every day, sometimes even when the weather was bad. She stood in sleet and snow, waving, her nose running. Her dad had moved to West Virginia with some whore. Her mom was always out with one of her boyfriends. Mom's boyfriends were inter-changeable. They all chewed tobacco or dipped snuff. Tonya swore to herself she would never kiss a man who did such a nasty thing.

When she was fifteen, she stopped going to the overpass because guys kept ruining it by pulling over and climbing the hill to try to talk her into fucking them. Sometimes she did fuck them, but it wasn't really what she wanted. She wanted to wave; she wanted them to keep going. She never looked over her shoulder at cars or trucks that had already passed under the bridge. Her attention was always on the vehicle coming.

After a few hours of waving, as darkness began to fall, she would head for home. She would pump and pump her bike five miles, mostly uphill, and she'd pull the screen door open, let it slap shut behind her, and yell, "Moooommmmmm! I'm home!" But the house would be empty.

THE WEARY MOTEL

Twenty-five

The truck's front end shimmies; the steering wheel shakes violently in his fists. Dill pumps the accelerator to make the speedometer jump above eighty and to hear the engine's unhealthy roar, a growl full of coughs and pings and screeches.

He's passing through the sliver of West Virginia that pokes up like a knife between Ohio and Pennsylvania. Hours ago, he got past Pittsburgh and was well on his way to Philadelphia before he realized he didn't want to go east. The East is crowded and dirty. The West provides some space. Kansas and Oklahoma don't have many trees or hills. The roads are wide and straight.

The night is black and cold. The night could use a fire. An exploding pick-up truck maybe.

But it's not really night anymore. The world is still black, but it's early morning. Tuesday? Yeah. Driving west. Running from the sun.

Sunday. It was Sunday afternoon when Dawnell woke him up to meet those people.

"Get up, Daddy. Daddy, you got to get up now."

Dill worked hard to open his eyes. His head felt huge and wobbly, as if he were Goofy or Mickey or Snoopy at the Macy's Thanksgiving Day parade.

He still had his clothes on, mud and blood caked on them. His room smelled like a bottle of Jack Daniels. Lori's image floated in front of him, and his gut clenched like a fist.

"Some people are here you got to see," Dawnell said.

"Who?" He rubbed his eyes, the calluses on his hands rough on his face. The wind was blowing hard, rocking the trailer. He heard trees, their bare branches rattling.

"The Picks."

"The Picks? I don't know . . . ."

"Mr. Pick, Mrs. Pick, and Oral Pick."

"*Who?*"

"You don't know them. And Reverend Haywood is here, too. They're all in the living room."

"Reverend?" He looked at Dawnell. She had on a dress, pale blue with a white sash around her big stomach. He couldn't remember the last time he had seen her in a dress. "What time is it?"

"Two-thirty."

"What?"

"Two-thirty."

"Why they here?"

"Just come on." Dawnell took his arm and tugged. Dill was dizzy as he got up. She took his hand and held it tight until she had him in the living room with four strangers. A short guy about fifty-five in a dark suit and three bean-pole people with tow heads. *Bean-pole people* was what Dill automatically thought. They were a half foot taller than he was, even the woman, and skinny as flag poles. Dawnell didn't make introductions. She was behind him, moving away.

The strangers were all huddled together until the man in the suit stepped forward and offered his hand to Dill. "I am the Reverend Elvis L. Haywood of The Church of the Glorious Resurrection. I'm very pleased to meet you."

Dill shook hands limply, tried to think of something to say but couldn't.

"You look as though you had an accident," Haywood said.

Dill shrugged, looked down at his clothes. "I was doin' a little cow tippin' this mornin'."

"Oh." Haywood took a step back.

The bean-pole man's yellow shirt had a collar way too big for his skinny neck and a red tie that was too short. The bean-pole boy, a kid about Dawnell's age, had on a white shirt and a wide gaudy tie with palm trees on it. The woman was wearing what looked like an old prom dress, a red frilly thing, wrinkled and with stray threads everywhere. Her nose was hooked like a parrot's. She smiled nervously, and her top lip pulled way up above her gums. Her teeth were an ugly gray. Dill thought of Lori's beautiful smile, her teeth so white and straight. He thought of her tongue. His gut clenched again.

Dill said, "I guess this is some special occasion?"

They all gave each other looks.

Then the preacher started making introductions: "Mr. Adam Pick. His wife—Mrs. Diana Pick. Their son—Oral Pick."

Dill shook their hands, their fingers long and bony, their knuckles big. He thought the man and wife looked like they were brother and sister. Their tow heads made him think of albinos, incest, and West Virginia. He looked to see if the Picks had pink eyes, but their eyes were blue.

"The Picks are members of my congregation."

In addition to the pain in his gut, it felt like somebody had stuck a knife in his head and was twisting it. The image of Lori still floated before him. "What's this all about?" Dill asked. "I'm sorry, folks, but if you're wantin' me to join your church . . . ."

Haywood and the Picks all looked at each other again. Mrs. Pick stopped smiling. Dawnell had disappeared. Mr. Pick cleared his throat and said, "I'll tell him, Reverend." He stepped toward Dill, his head lifted, his eyes on the low ceiling, his Adam's apple big as a golf ball. Then he looked Dill in the eyes. "My boy Oral here has got your girl . . . in the family way."

Dill sat down on the sofa.

Haywood put his hand on Dill's shoulder. "The boy wants to do the right thing, the only thing. Right, Oral?"

"Yes, sir." He nodded his head hard, his long chin bouncing off his chest.

Dill looked at the boy. The kid's face was pink and smooth, his eyebrows white.

"They're getting married as soon as possible," Haywood said.

Dill had been waking up gradually. Now that he was fairly alert he realized they all must have been thinking he was in shock over Dawnell being pregnant. And he was. It *was* a sur-

prise. It *was* a shock, but there was something that, for the
moment, overpowered that shock: he couldn't get the image of Lori
out of his head, the image of her below him the last time he made
love to her—and he couldn't stop thinking that he'd like to see her
dead.

The low, barely audible whine of hillbilly music comes out
of the truck's radio.

This morning—no, yesterday morning—Monday—Dill
went to The Harrison Family Dental Clinic, walked right past the
buck-toothed receptionist and into a room where Lori was drilling
the hell out of some old lady in a flower-print dress. The drill's
whine cut the air. Dill smelled smoke.

When Lori saw him, she froze, the drill suddenly dead,
the color suddenly gone from her face.

The old lady had her eyes closed, and her jaw was slack.
Her two big circles of rouge on her cheeks and her smeared
bright-red lipstick reminded Dill of a whore he knew in Texas
years ago who advertised herself in the newspaper as "locally
trained masseuse with fifty years of experience." The old lady in
Lori's dental chair groaned and rolled her head back and forth.
Dill opened his mouth but couldn't talk. He had decided to kill
Lori. Maybe. Probably with his bare hands. It was a vague plan,
but he knew he had to see her, to at least hurt her—because she
was hurting him.

But as soon as he saw her, he couldn't keep hold of the
anger. He stared at her, studied her. She wore a light-blue smock
and had her hair pulled back into a bun and was wearing her
glasses. The smock hid her heavy breasts. She looked tired. He
wanted to make love to her. He didn't feel like killing her, but he
held the hope for a moment that she might soon die of breast
cancer.

Her husband entered the room cautiously, the receptionist
behind him with her eyes bugging out, her big front teeth hanging
over her lip. "He just stormed right past me, Harry...ah, Doctor...."

"What's going on?" the husband said to the whole room,
not to Dill directly.

Dill studied him. He had never seen him up close. In
addition to the orange hair and pale skin, he had freckles. Dill

looked at Lori. She started to say something but looked at her husband and stopped, and Dill thought he could sense some kind of silent communication taking place. Then the guy looked at Dill, looked him over, his eyes pausing on the blood stains on the front of Dill's jeans.

Dill suddenly felt calm. His face stopped burning. He'd been sweating, and now he felt chilled. He decided he was going to stop acting like a maniac. He didn't really want to hurt anybody. He still loved Lori. He would handle all this with grace and dignity. He said, "I guess I got the wrong day." As he walked past Harry, he mumbled, "Dentist's office always makes me nervous." Dill laughed like a lunatic for a few seconds, shivered, pushed open the front door of the clinic. His boots slid on the gravel of the parking lot. His knees hurt.

Getting into his truck, he felt good about himself, proud of the way he was handling things. He felt sentimental about his relationship with Lori. He could sympathize with her pathetic orange-headed husband. Dill was full of affection and understanding for Lori.

Within five minutes, he again wanted to kill her. He was roaring down the Appalachian Highway, and he made himself keep going.

Dill now understands all those nuts he's heard about on the news, men who killed their wives or girlfriends, then themselves. When you want something bad enough, you can't bear knowing that it exists and isn't yours, that you can never have it, that you have no control over it, that it could fall into the hands of somebody else.

Somebody named Bruce. It . . . it—

It? Her. *Her.*

The whore.

After you blow her head off, you *have* to kill yourself, too, because you're a problem to yourself, as much a problem as she was. You eliminate both problems.

He scares himself with how seriously he's thinking of smashing the truck into a guardrail or jumping the median strip and steering into the headlights of a tractor-trailer.

Sometimes, the thought of nothingness is the sweetest thing he can imagine. When he drinks enough cherry wine, he always passes out with little warning. It's a nice surprise—that nothingness sneaking up on him, then wrapping itself around him. Sweet blackness. No feeling at all, a sweet thing beyond numbness. To be taken by that and carried away, to disappear, to be added to the list of "missing." Sweet. A gift.

Jesus, he's got to snap out of it. He turns up the radio. More hillbilly whining. But he likes it.

Where is he? A sign appears: WELCOME TO OHIO, THE BUCKEYE STATE.

He wants to cry again. Dawnell has often made him feel the urge to cry the last couple of years, but he hasn't cried since Carol got killed. Suddenly, he's missing Carol, wanting Carol, more than he has in years.

He thinks about how he couldn't come the last time he and Carol made love. It was a Sunday afternoon, and he had already made love to her four times since they woke up that morning. They had gone to McDonald's for breakfast, and they had joked about how there must have been something in the sausage biscuits that turned people into sex maniacs.

They were desperate for each other that day; they couldn't get enough of each other. It was the first of June, hot and humid, and they didn't have an air conditioner. He and Carol were slick and shiny with sweat. Her hair was a mess of tangles. His penis was raw, but he didn't want to stop until he came again.

Finally, they had to stop because Dawnell woke up in her crib and started screaming. The next day, Carol got herself killed.

One of his crazy thoughts: dig up Carol. Yes. Go to the cemetery and dig her up.

Jesus. What for?

He doesn't know. He just has the overwhelming desire to dig. To get her back. Get her back. Get sixteen back, to be sixteen and have all that stupid, blind, senseless hope.

Cry. He wishes he could cry. Wash these crazy thoughts from his head.

The truck roars through the night, taking him back toward Adams County. The radio gets louder as he races toward home. He drives faster—ninety, ninety-five. He didn't know his truck could do it. The whole truck shimmies, rattles. Dill envisions parts flying off—the hood lifting up and tumbling over the cab, the side-view mirrors screeching loose from their bolts, the headlights exploding, the front bumper dropping to the road to be immediately smashed like a fat snake by the truck's tires, the tires then exploding and the truck roaring along on the metal rims. Lord, the racket he'll be making as he presses on, his foot crushing the accelerator—he'll wake the dead.

The radio gets louder and louder.

Home. He's got to get home to his baby, to Dawnell. His baby is going to have a baby. His baby is getting married.

Something on the radio—he just missed it.

What? Something about the Pumpkin Festival Queen. Something about her being found? Something about . . . tattoos?

He eases off the accelerator, turns the radio down to reduce the static. The voice on the radio is announcing grain prices.

Dawnell is going to have a baby. Dill opens his mouth, lets out a moan and a sob.

Tears pour.

THE WEARY MOTEL

Twenty-six

Drew is hopping around the barnyard, trying to keep warm and singing loudlly, "ORAL AND DAWNELL. . . SITTIN' IN A TREEEEEEE. . . K-I-S-S-I-N-G. . .FIRST COMES LOVE. . . ." His breath chugs out of him like smoke from the giant bulldozers that strip mine the hills across the river in Kentucky.

Oral sets, his knees bent, his fingers splayed under and behind the basketball, his head up, his eyes riveted to the netless hoop bolted to the weathered barn, and he shoots. The ball drops onto the rim, spins, falls the wrong way.

Oral retrieves the ball, turns quickly, and shoots about a yard too far to the left. Drew, Oral's fourteen-year-old brother, smirks, says, "So like does *Dog*nell scream, 'Give it to me, big boy,' when you're doin' it to her, or does she just snort like a pig?"

Drew is a foot shorter than Oral but twice as broad and thick. Mysteriously, Drew doesn't look a thing like Dad, Mom, Oral, or their sister, Nancy.

Oral's next shot falls short of the hoop. He sighs, his ears and face burning from the cold. His lungs ache.

Loving Dawnell is the only thing he's good at, he figures. But that's enough. Probably. Because she's pregnant, his parents keep bitching about him ruining his life, but he doesn't think so. Last night his mother was crying and said, "You'll never ripen into a real man now." Oral wonders what the hell that means.

Drew has the ball. He shoots, and the ball whacks the

hoop hard and the hoop vibrates. "Cool," Drew says.

Although Oral's fingers and face ache from the cold, he doesn't want to sit inside the house with his parents. The place is so damn small. He and Drew have bunk beds, and Nancy sleeps just a few feet away on the other side of the room. Down the short hall, on the other side of the bathroom, is Mom and Dad's room. And there's the living room and kitchen, but that's it. The house seems to have gotten smaller in the last couple of years. Now Oral knows how the hamster he used to have felt when it grew too big for its cage and could barely turn around in it.

There's no peace, and nowhere to go except outdoors. His mother often reminds him that she carried him in her womb for eleven months, a circumstance that in itself makes him feel like puking, but he's also bitter because if he hadn't been born late he'd be sixteen now and would have his driver's license.

He keeps reminding himself that his life is in transition, and this thought—this fact—makes him feel better. He has an older woman, one with a driver's license, and whose dad owns a twelve-unit motel. He and Dawnell are going to have their own room to live in, and they're going to keep the place clean and fixed up. Twelve rooms. Plus the office. Easy work and he'll feel like he's living in a mansion.

In their pen next to the barn, the hogs rut and snort. Two of them are fighting over an ear of horse corn. Oral hates pigs, hates farming. He made up his mind when he was seven that he wouldn't be a farmer.

He sets, tries to concentrate, shoots again, misses. Won't be a basketball player either, though. His parents thought that because he was tall he might be able to play, but they were wrong. Dad put up the hoop on the barn when Oral was twelve, but Dad put it too high. It's about thirteen feet from the ground. Oral kind of likes fooling around shooting baskets by himself. Sometimes he doesn't mind Drew shooting with him as long as Drew doesn't talk, but Oral hates playing basketball at school during phys-ed class. The teacher makes the boys play Shirts and Skins. Oral hates to be on Skins because of his sunken, pale chest and bony back. Neither side ever wants him. Except for Tubs Morton, Oral always gets picked last.

But, boy, what he's done now is a shock to Adams County

and the world. Ripe is exactly what he already is. Boy, ripe at fifteen—he's gotten a girl pregnant. Nobody expected him to be so sinful. Nobody expected him to be such a stud.

Drew seems to be dancing to some weird music in his head.

Oral says, "Why don't you go inside if you're so cold."

"I ain't cold. Did Mom tell you you're gettin' married at Dognell's aunt's house?"

"Yeah."

"I heard Mom on the phone a long time with her aunt. They got a piano, so Nancy's gonna play. Great, huh? Hey, let me shoot it."

Oral takes another shot, makes it, and Drew grabs the ball; his feet spin on the frozen ground, and he shoots, misses.

"Nancy's gonna play?" Oral says. "She'll ruin my wedding."

The hogs are squealing again. Steam rises from their fresh feces.

Nancy, who's ten, practices on an ancient out-of-tune upright Mom bought for fifty dollars last year. The thing takes up half the living room. It had been painted black before Mom bought it. The keys are all yellow, and half of them are cracked. Mom thought Nancy might have talent because she has incredibly long, slim fingers. That's another one of his parents' dreams down the drain. At least they're realistic about Drew. Dad calls him "Shit Brain" more than he calls him Drew.

Drew shoots and makes it, then tosses the ball to Oral. "What you think it's going to be like having a kid?"

"Huh?" Oral freezes in mid-pivot. The ball slips from his hands, rolls over the hard ground toward the hog pen.

"I'll be an uncle, won't I? I just thought of that. Boy, that's gonna be weird." Drew's running to get the basketball. "I'm too young to be a uncle. Hey, you ever meet Dognell's aunt? She fat, too?"

Oral mumbles, "Looks ain't everything."

"Huh?"

"Nothin'."

"What?"

"I said looks ain't everything." He looks around at the

landscape—the barren tobacco patch and the black, naked trees
and the brown stubbly corn field. The sky is blue and looks as
hard as any ceiling, strong enough to support the bulk of a God big
as a professional wrestler. Mom says God punishes wickedness.
Oral looks up and awaits mutilation. Death.

     Drew says, "I'm goin' in. How 'bout you?"

     "I guess."

     Oral hangs his coat on the back of the kitchen door.
Down in the basement the furnace chugs, and hot air blows up
through the floor registers. Mom is molding ground beef into a
meat loaf. Her long slender hands shake as she reaches for the
pepper—maybe because Nancy's banging out the wedding march
on the piano, getting maybe half the notes right, and Dad has
"Gilligan's Island" turned up loud. Oral moves slowly through the
kitchen, feeling like a ghost because his mother acts as though she
can't see him.

     Dad is in his green vinyl lounger. The seat of the chair
bears a permanent impression of Dad's butt. As Dad laughs, his
paunch swells and jiggles. Because of the way Dad's small, pink
mouth hangs open, Oral suspects that the old man has a thing for
Mary Ann and Ginger. Drew has plopped down at Dad's feet.
Dad's cigarette smoke mingles with the smells of greasy foods, the
furnace, Nancy's cheap perfume. Dad's eyes don't even shift when
Oral passes through the room.

     Oral goes to his and Drew's and Nancy's room, closes the
door, and climbs up onto the top bunk. On the ceiling is a school
photo of Dawnell. She's frowning. She always frowns, but he likes
that about her. Kids at school are always laughing like hyenas.
They're always laughing at some dumb joke or at somebody. They
laugh when they punch him or when they pinch him and he cries
out and when they stuff him into a locker, slamming the door on
his nose and his fingers. Last spring three boys laughed like
hyenas as they dunked his head in a toilet. Somebody had written
on the stall, "Oral Pick blows horses. I have proof!"

     As he rolls onto his stomach, a familiar sinking feeling
pushes his face into the pillow. Being married to Dawnell and
working at her dad's motel is probably going to suck. Life sucks.
He sees a motel floor littered with cigarette butts, beer cans, and
rubbers. He can smell the smoke, the beer, and the sex. He sees

Dawnell's pear-shaped, flabby body.

He rolls over with a grunt and glares at the white ceiling until the images and smells fade.

Yeah, he hates giggly girls. Even at church, the girls are always giggling. He likes Dawnell's frown, and he likes knowing that no one else wants her. No one will ever try to steal her away from him.

He closes his eyes, sees stars, smells meat loaf and Drew's dirty socks.

Oral's eyelids feel heavy.

Three times.

He and Dawnell have had sex only three times. Always at her mobile home when her dad was gone. She drove him there after school. Her tiny room was decorated with pictures of her dead mother and dead rock stars and dead actors. Now she will be his wife. Forever. They'll have all those rooms.

Only three times. And *bam!* Man, he is some kind of stud, as ripe as a man can get.

Man, life is going to be good for a change, he thinks as he drifts into a dream about bright red cherries, yellow pears, golden apples falling from the sky and turning into basketballs that *whoosh* the net.

THE WEARY MOTEL

Twenty-seven

Jo Rene picks up Grandma from the nursing home the night before the wedding. Grandma is in a quiet mood. She sits on the sofa, drinks a Coke, and watches old reruns of "My Three Sons," "The Mister Ed Show," "Donna Reed," and "Alfred Hitchcock" on Nickelodeon. Dawnell shows up during "Alfred Hitchcock" to spend the night here, too. She has a yellow dress wadded in her fist.

"I'll iron it for you," Jo Rene says. "This will be real pretty."

Dawnell grunts, watches TV for a few minutes, then says she's going up to bed.

Grandma watches "I Love Lucy" next. Jo Rene keeps looking over at her and studying the lines in her face, the way her flesh sags and the way light comes and goes in her eyes.

Later, Jo Rene helps her up the stairs to the room Grandma slept in for sixty years and makes sure she doesn't have any trouble getting into her nightgown. She tucks Grandma in, kisses her cheek. Grandma hasn't said more than two words all evening.

But in the middle of the night Jo Rene hears noises downstairs and finds Grandma dusting, making slow circles with a soft rag on top of the side-board in the dining room.

"I dusted just last week," Jo Rene says.

"Isn't somebody getting married?"

"Yeah."

"Then we need to dust again."

Jo Rene shrugs and decides to mop the kitchen floor.

When Grandma finishes dusting, Jo Rene coaxes her back to bed. Grandma gets under the ancient quilt Great-grandma made eighty years ago out of scraps of Grandma's and Willy's and Great-grandpa's worn-out clothes.

"We have a big day tomorrow," Jo Rene says.

"I never thought Jo Rene would get married."

Jo Rene stares at a faded rose on Grandma's wallpaper above her ornately carved headboard. "Grandma, Dawnell is the one getting married. *I'm* Jo Rene."

"Better tell her about the birds and the bees."

"I think Dawnell already knows."

Grandma's eyes light up. "Is she knocked up?"

Jo Rene can't help smiling. "She's in the family way, Grandma."

"I was, too, when I married your grandpa. I don't care if you know. I'll be dead soon."

"Oh, Grandma . . . ." Jo Rene giggles nervously, foolishly. "You've got lots of time."

"Jesus Christ, girl, I'm ninety-one years old. By the way, how old is Dawnell?"

"Sixteen."

"You know, my mother gave me a book to read when I was sixteen. *Confidential Conversations with Young Women*, it was called. Written by some doctor. Can't remember much except that he talked a lot about ovaries and God's plans." She pulls the quilt up higher around her neck. "I'm cold. Damn cold."

"I'll turn up the furnace." Jo Rene moves toward the door.

Grandma looks thinner since moving to the nursing home. Jo Rene remembers being a kid and Grandma saying, "I don't like being old, but I guess it's better than the alternative." At the time, Jo Rene thought the alternative was being young and stupid. When she suddenly realized one day that the alternative was death, she shivered with disgust the way she did when in seventh grade Joy Johnston told her that boys' peters got hard as steel. "Harder than this desk," Joy said somberly and rapped her wooden desk top with her knuckles.

 "Jo Rene?"

 "Yes, Grandma?"

 "Have you heard from Scott or Kari?"

 "No."

 "Come here and hug me."

THE WEARY MOTEL

Twenty-eight

There wasn't room at the office for the antiques, and besides, the office building was such a tacky little thing really, the low flat roof and the ugly pale brick, the product of the early sixties' tastes and a mediocre architect's idea of practicality. When she and Harry bought the building for their dental practice, it had blue shag carpeting throughout and wallpaper with bold vertical strips of gold and silver, and the rooms were full of old metal filing cabinets and metal desks with simulated wood-grain veneers. What a nightmare. The place had first served as the offices for an insurance agency, then a mortgage company, then some kind of mail-order business.

So she and Harry decided to decorate a room of their 1817 stone mansion with the antiques—a dental chair (circa 1890), a dental drill (circa 1910), a dentist's stool (circa 1900), and a tray of dental instruments—pliers, clamps, probes (circa 1895). The instruments are rusty and pointed, look like instruments of torture. They make Lori imagine dungeons, mad scientists (or dentists), and she laughs.

She lies in the dental chair. Its leather is faded and cracked, but the stuffing is not coming out anywhere. It's really in very good shape and was an excellent buy.

It's late and Lori's exhausted. The girls are at a slumber party. Harry is out somewhere. He said he just wanted to take a drive by himself. He's still a bit upset about yesterday—Dill coming into the office and all. But Harry will get over it. At this very moment he probably has some buckteeth wrapped around his skinny cock.

She is waiting for the cordless phone in her lap to ring. She brought the phone in here from the kitchen because the only phone in this room is a 1909 wooden crank model on the wall next to the 1872 roll-top desk.

She wishes Bruce would hurry and call. She hasn't talked to him in days. She can tell him about Dill being mean and scaring her. Bruce is a good listener, the best listener of any of the men she's loved, and she's certain that she loves Bruce more than she's ever loved anyone.

Bruce likes opera. And maybe it's silly, she knows, but that kind of thing is important. Harry would go to the opera, but he never closed his eyes and swayed his head while absorbing an aria the way Bruce does.

And as for Dill . . . well, Dill didn't get it at all. When she took him to Cincinnati to see *The Merry Widow*, he kept fidgeting and tugging at his tie. He whispered, "What's the deal with the baron's wife and the guy puttin' the moves on her?"

Lori said, "Oh, she's a slut." And Dill looked at her like she had said something bizarre. Yeah, sure, Lori knew she wasn't the perfect wife herself, but . . . well, it was different.

During the intermission after act one, Dill left her alone and walked down the street and bought a six pack of beer to get him through acts two and three.

It was worse when she made him go see *Madam Butterfly*. He hissed three times, "*What* language is this?" *Madam Butterfly* always made Lori cry.

Dill asked her whether she had a pen in her purse. Then he took it and started drawing on her arm. She felt like wringing his neck and throwing his corpse over the railing of the balcony. "I'm givin' you a tattoo," he breathed in her ear. Usually she liked his hot breath on her neck or in her ear, but this time it just annoyed her, like some strange cat jumping into her lap. "I ever tell you," he whispered loudly, "that I like women with tattoos?"

The beautiful music washed over her, but the pen point tickled her upper arm, distracted her to no end. "Stop it!" she said too loud. Men's heads turned in their stiff collars, and women's diamond necklaces flashed as they twisted their necks. Dill had drawn a heart on her arm with "Dill" inside, as if it never occurred to him that her husband would see it unless she spent a half hour in the ladies room scrubbing the ink away.

Dill had her, though. He knew she hated to draw negative attention to herself. Now that she had received a dozen dirty looks, she couldn't make another peep.

Dill held her arm firmly and drew a snake and the words "Don't tread on me."

Bruce, on the other hand, is like a Victorian gentleman. Lori giggles, lying in her antique dental chair. God, is she silly or what? Tonight is one of those times when a drink would be nice, just one glass of sherry. She met Bruce at an AA meeting. Right away, she liked his expensive suits, his clean-cut good looks, his impeccable manners, his high income, his good vocabulary, and the curve of his thick penis.

She is already starting to forget what she liked about Dill. She just hopes he stays away. Maybe she's cruel, but she can't help it. She just can't help it. She's just trying to be happy.

The phone in her lap rings.

The Weary Motel

Twenty-nine

Jo Rene's alarm goes off, and she awakes with the feeling she's going to be worn out all day if she gets up now, but she still has a lot to do to get things ready for the wedding.

Shuffling down the hall in her slippers and robe, she stops at the door of the extra bedroom, expecting to hear Dawnell snorting and snoring but hears crying instead. She presses her ear against the door, then knocks. She waits. The crying continues.

She opens the door slowly and peeks in. Dawnell is sitting up in bed, her hair a greasy-looking tangle. Jo Rene sits down on the edge of the bed and says, "Everybody gets cold feet at the last minute." Jo Rene looks over at the window and adds, "Least that's what I hear."

Dawnell shakes her head. She isn't wearing a nightgown or pajamas. Apparently, she slept in her jeans and the shirt she had on last night. Dawnell smells like cigarette smoke, and Jo Rene wonders whether she should suggest that she wash her hair. After all, it *is* a special occasion. "I'm just happy," Dawnell says.

"Oh. Well, good." Jo Rene looks back at Dawnell. "Oral sounds like a nice boy."

That's what Dill said: "He seems like a nice kid. A dork but a nice boy." Jo Rene hasn't even seen Oral yet. She's just talked to his mother on the phone.

"I *think* I'm happy." Dawnell turns her head toward the window. "Nobody else would ever want me." Her flannel shirt is bunched up and reveals a slab of flesh at her waist.

Jo Rene doesn't know what to say. She agrees—probably nobody else would ever want her—but she doesn't say so. "You want to talk? I mean, really talk about things?"

"What things?"

"I don't know. Important things. Love. Sex. Relationships." Jo Rene shrugs.

"No."

"Okay. If you do . . . ."

Dawnell nods, her bad complexion streaked with tears.

Jo Rene goes down into the kitchen. She has to figure out how many little triangular sandwiches she needs for the reception. And how much punch. And how many slices of Partridge Farm chocolate cake for the people who won't want the white wedding cake. The other day, after Dill told her Dawnell was going to have to get married, Jo Rene suggested that the wedding be at Grandma's house. It would be much nicer than that tacky church called the something something of the Resurrection or the VFW hall, where a lot of people have receptions.

Mom, Howard (maybe), Marilyn Thompson, Reverend Haywood, Mr. Pick, Mrs. Pick, Oral, his sister, his brother, Dawnell, Grandma, Dill. How many sandwiches could that many people eat? Oh, and herself.

She decides she'll make some of the sandwiches with cheese spread on them, some with peanut butter, some with ham spread. Later, she will have to pick up the wedding cake from the bakery in Peebles. She ordered one with a plastic bride and groom on top, the little figures standing inside a pink heart. For a minute she stands frozen, holding a knife smeared with cheese spread and thinks of Buck.

Then she snaps out of her trance and goes into the living room to turn on the TV so that she can listen to it while she works.

"Adams County's Pumpkin Festival Queen is no longer missing," says a Cincinnati newswoman. "Authorities have confirmed that Heather Burns is safe and well in Knoxville, Tennessee."

Jo Rene sits down on the sofa. The newswoman doesn't look real, is as pretty as a mannequin. A picture of Heather Burns appears on the screen.

Heather is all right. She is a total stranger to Jo Rene, but tears are suddenly in Jo Rene's eyes, and her throat aches.

The newswoman explains that Heather was recognized in a Knoxville tattoo parlor by a truck driver from Adams County. She was there with her boyfriend.

Now there's a blurry picture of the boyfriend—a beefy, long-haired guy straddling a motorcycle. They were getting tattoo wedding rings.

The picture of Heather reappears. She is dressed in a pink formal, her blonde hair done up fancy on her head, not a stray strand anywhere, her smile big and white like she could make a fortune doing toothpaste commercials, a pumpkin decorated with gold streamers in her slim arms.

Recorded earlier, Heather's parents share their feelings. Frail, gray, and with a front tooth missing, the mother says, "We just thank the good lord she's all right." The stepfather, bald and pig-eyed, says, "I told everybody from the start she probably run off with that Jake boy."

The sheriff appears, the camera tight on his moon face: "I'm glad she has not been a victim of foul play, don't get me wrong, but we spent over $40,000 looking for this young woman. Lives were placed in danger . . . ."

Jo Rene sniffs, tries to reconcile The Pumpkin Festival Queen in all her formal beauty with ugly parents, a biker, and tattoos.

Sure. Why not?

She thinks tattoos are tacky, but she kind of likes the idea of tattoo wedding rings. You can't take them off, and that's very romantic.

She gets off the sofa and looks out the window. Ice has formed in the corners of the panes. The sky is bright blue. The weatherman is on now. The temperature is five above zero. The high will be around fifteen. Still, Jo Rene's heart is warmed by the discovery of The Pumpkin Queen, the idea of tattoo wedding rings, and the thought of a wedding in Grandma's house.

She notices the mailman coming up the driveway.

THE WEARY MOTEL

Thirty

Jo Rene knows that some time soon, maybe any second now, she is going to scream or faint. The two postcards that the old mailman delivered this morning are disintegrating in her sweaty hands.

In the living room, Oral's little sister is massacring "Here Comes the Bride," but it's not as bad as the Mozart and Beethoven she was attempting earlier. Mrs. Pick got excited when Jo Rene told her about Grandma's old Wurlitzer. Mrs. Pick's voice came out of the phone faster and louder. "We thought we might as well use Oral's wedding as a chance to debut Nancy's piano talents."

Dawnell and Jo Rene are in the dining room, standing by the entrance into the living room. "I ain't goin' in there," Dawnell says. "I want my daddy."

"What?" Jo Rene looks at the postcards again. One has a picture of a Las Vegas casino on it; the other shows lightning striking in the night all over Albuquerque, New Mexico.

"Where's Dill?" Dawnell says. "Where's my daddy?"

Dill is upstairs in the bathroom. He's embarrassed because he can't stop crying. Jo Rene says, "You know how he is."

"Where is he?"

"I'll go try to get him."

Jo Rene talks through the bathroom door. "Dill, we can't do this without you."

She has to wait awhile before he says, "Okay. I'll be there in a minute."

Jo Rene returns to Dawnell, who's half singing, half mumbling, "Had me a girl in Kalamazoo, she sure knew . . . how to screw . . . ."

"What?"

"Nothin'."

"Your daddy's coming."

"Yeah, sure."

On the Las Vegas postcard, "Jo Rene" is spelled as one word, "Jorene." Other than her name and address (no zip code) are only the words "Arrive soon" scrawled in pencil. At first, she thought Kari had done the writing. On the Albuquerque card the postmark is a day later. The writing is the same scrawl. The message is "Arrive sooner or later day after morrow."

Nancy Pick, done up in light blue frills and with three bows in her almost-white blonde hair, bangs away. All the people in the living room are craning their necks to see why Dawnell doesn't come in, walk to the Christmas tree, and take her place beside Oral, in front of Reverend Haywood.

Nancy finishes "Here Comes the Bride" with a long last wrong note. There's silence for a moment. Then Haywood says, "Play it again, Nancy, please."

Marilyn Thompson, Dawnell's maid of honor, a big girl with a runny nose, stands near Haywood, fiddling with the corsage pinned to the front of her green dress.

Oral's face is bright red and streaked with sweat, although Grandma's old furnace barely keeps them all from freezing. His head trembles, gives little jerky shakes, as if he were a hundred years old. His best man, his brother Drew, sneers over at Nancy and mutters, "Try playin' some of the right notes, turd face."

Mrs. Pick shoots Drew a dirty look. "We all want to hear it again, Nancy honey," she says. Mrs. Pick seemed to Jo Rene kind of shy and sweet at first and grateful for Jo Rene's offer to host the wedding, but it didn't take her long to get bossy about how things should be done.

Nancy sticks her tongue out at Drew, starts banging away, and says loudly, "Dick head."

"Get me outta this dress!" Dawnell says, tugging at the

big white sash at her waist. Everybody hears her and stares. Haywood is grinning and nodding, motioning for Dawnell to come to him, but she heads the other way, into the kitchen. Jo Rene follows in a panic.

"What's wrong?"

"I changed my mind. Is my face breakin' out worse?"

"Well, yeah, you got some new pimples it looks like, but—"

"It's a sign."

"I thought you loved him."

"Could *you* love somebody named Oral Pick? He's only a Goddamn sophomore. He gets beat up every other day and stuffed in lockers. Would you want a husband that got stuffed in lockers? And he's losin' his hair."

"I didn't notice—I don't see—"

"I want a real man that's not gonna go bald."

Jo Rene feels impatient. She blows out a big sigh. "For one thing, I don't think Sylvester Stallone is going to be coming through Peebles, Ohio, any time soon. For another thing, you got a baby to think about."

Dawnell's yellow dress—covered with ribbons and lace— and her heavy make-up, which Marilyn Thompson helped her apply, make her look like a lady TV evangelist or a whacked-out hooker.

When the piano stops again, there's snoring. Grandma. Jo Rene goes to the entrance to the living room and looks in, and everybody stares at her accusingly. Grandma's black hat with a veil has slipped cock-eyed on her head, and she has slumped against Mr. Pick on the sofa. He looks as though he needs to be rescued. Mrs. Pick looks pissed. Jo Rene reads her mind: *Hasn't that fat girl made enough trouble already?*

In a chair on the other side of the room, Mom has picked up a *People* magazine off the coffee table and is reading. Howard didn't come.

In a voice suggesting great weariness, Drew says, "Play it again, turd face."

"That will be enough of that, young man," explodes Mrs. Pick. "You open your trap one more time, just one more time. Boy, I will slap that grin off your face if it's not gone in one second."

Marilyn Thompson says, "Reverend, you think I could sit down. I'm gettin' light headed."

Haywood ignores her. "A problem?" he says to Jo Rene, but Jo Rene can't get any words out to describe what's happening. "Miss Jenkins?"

"Hormones!" Jo Rene blurts out.

Dill finally descends the stairs. His eyes and nose are red. His red tie is crooked. He nods to Haywood. "I'll see about things, Reverend."

In the kitchen, Dill says to Dawnell, "Don't you want to no more?"

"I don't know."

Jo Rene asks, "What do you want, Dawnell?"

"I want everybody to leave me alone."

"Do you love this boy?" Dill asks softly. Then he starts crying again.

Dawnell stares at Dill for what seems like a long time, then takes his arm. "Walk me in there."

They enter the living room, Dawnell trembling, her ankles collapsing on her white high heels. Dill places her between Marilyn and Oral and takes a step back, looks down at the floor, his shoulders shaking. Grandma is awake, blinking hard. Jo Rene stands in the doorway, her fingers rubbing the postcards into dust.

Haywood clears his throat. "We are here today to witness the holy union of these two young people, Dawnell Carolyn Jenkins and Oral Peabody Pick—"

Dawnell throws up her arms. "Fuck this shit!" She heads toward the front door. Oral sends up a wail: "Dawneeeeeellll!"

She turns, stares at the Christmas tree while pointing at Oral, and says to everyone, "I'm not spendin' my life at The Weary Motel." Then she continues toward the front door—awfully fast, Jo Rene thinks, for a big girl.

Mrs. Pick tries to trip Dawnell, but she only stumbles. Dawnell reaches the front door, flings it open. Arctic air hits the room like an atomic blast. Jo Rene runs to the door, opens her mouth. After a few seconds, something comes unstuck in her throat, and she screams like a girl in a horror movie as Dawnell climbs into her Gremlin. The engine catches. The car lurches.

Dawnell bumps down the driveway, then out onto the road—gone with a roar. Finally, Jo Rene stops screaming.

Almost right away, another car pulls into the driveway and heads toward the house. It approaches slowly, a tiny red Fiat. It pulls up in front of the house. Jo Rene's teeth are chattering.

Scott pops out of the car, looks around at all the other vehicles in the yard, and says, "Are we here just in time for a party or what?"

THE WEARY MOTEL

Thirty-one

Jo Rene holds her sleeping baby on her lap. Kari was asleep when Scott drove up two hours ago. She woke up long enough to give Jo Rene a weak hug and say, "I love you." Then she dropped off again.

Scott is across the room, casual as can be, a real actor. He doesn't act at all like the criminal he is. He's talking to Mr. Pick and Reverend Haywood, who both have big grins and seem to think they're actually socializing with a celebrity. Scott has already done a short Elvis impersonation for them—a few bars of "Jail House Rock"—and one of Glen Campbell singing "Wichita Lineman."

"You know if you're in the area one Sunday next summer," Haywood says to Scott, "you'll have to come to Sunday service and then to my house for barbecue."

"I'd like that Reverend. I'd like that a lot."

"Really? You would?" Haywood grins like a madman.

Jo Rene rocks Kari, and tears come to her eyes for about the twentieth time. Holding Kari seems like a miracle. The little girl is worn out from three days of riding in the car. All the way from Reno, Scott said. Only God knows if that's really where they were.

Scott must be on those pills, those uppers, he has always taken. He claims he hasn't slept since leaving Nevada, and he acts wired. He's babbling something to Pick and Haywood—his audience—about playing poker with Wayne Newton and Shawn Cassidy.

Jo Rene squeezes Kari, who snores softly, her breath hot on Jo Rene's neck. Grandma is asleep, too, over in a chair.

Mom left half an hour ago, making the excuse that she just couldn't stay any longer because she had promised Howard she'd go out with him tonight. As she drove away, Jo Rene noticed little mechanical bull dogs in the back window of the Buick bobbing their heads and a new bumper sticker on the trunk lid: "51% sweetie, 49% bitch. Don't push it."

Mrs. Pick has taken her three children into Peebles to the McDonald's, even though Jo Rene had all those little sandwiches prepared, which are now getting stale. Before they left, Drew and Nancy were exchanging put downs and trying to shove each other off the piano bench. Oral was lying on the sofa, rolling his head and mumbling as if he were in a fever: "I been stood up at the altar. I can't believe it. I been stood up at the altar."

Mrs. Pick said, "Come on, Oral. I'll take you to McDonald's. Maybe Dawnell will be here when we get back."

"Yeah," Drew said, "maybe *Dog*nell will be back."

Dill left shortly after Dawnell did to look for her at home and at the motel and to try to talk some sense into her. But Jo Rene doesn't know; she just doesn't know. Maybe Dawnell has the right idea running away. She could have the baby without marrying Oral. Jo Rene has managed without a husband. She smooths Kari's hair, kisses her head.

Jo Rene looks across the room again at Scott. Reverend Haywood is saying, "You ever meet a lady preacher out there named Gloria Duncan? I've watched her on cable. Has a big hairdo and bad teeth?"

Kari stirs, turns, mumbles, drools. She is *so* big. She seems to have grown a foot and gained twenty pounds. Jo Rene has been inspecting her for scars, bruises, sores, but has found nothing. She keeps feeling her forehead for a fever. When Scott lifted her out of the car, she was wearing a pink snowsuit. He told Jo Rene he bought it in Tulsa about the time they hit the frigid weather.

Jo Rene wonders whether she should call the sheriff and try to get Scott tossed in jail. She really does hate him. She really has, all these months, wanted to see him dead, but now killing him seems like too much trouble. She doesn't have the energy. Maybe she'll call the sheriff after she gets over the shock of him just showing up this way.

"Bob Hope is a beautiful man," Scott says to his awed listeners.

Pick and Haywood have no idea they're listening to a kidnaper and the biggest liar who ever lived in Adams County, Ohio. Suddenly, Scott sees Jo Rene glaring at him and excuses himself and comes over to her. He nods at Kari.

"She's grown up a lot."

Jo Rene nods. Tears well up again.

"Yeah. She's over Luke Perry. She loves Tom Cruise now. Where's the guy with one hand?"

"I ought to cut your balls off, you son of a bitch."

Pick and Haywood look over at her.

"I'm her daddy," Scott says.

"So? You just did this to hurt me." She squeezes Kari, inhales the scent of her baby.

He shrugs. "You know, you look good."

"You're insane."

He shrugs again. "You do. You look mighty good. I started missing you big time."

"You can miss me some more while you're in prison. I'm going to call the FBI." She glares at his Nike tennis shoes.

Scott goes over to the dining-room table where the food is laid out and picks up a little sandwich made with cheese spread. He eats it in two bites and then comes back over to her.

"You know, Jo Rene, you're the only woman I've ever *really* loved."

"Don't start," she says wearily.

Then she does something dangerous. She looks into his eyes, and she waits to fall like a fool all over again. For a moment, only a moment, she feels the old pull. But it has lost its force. It's a weak tug, a mere memory of a sad weight on her heart.

ABOUT THE AUTHOR

Mark Spencer grew up on a farm in southern Ohio and now teaches creative writing at Cameron University in Lawton, Oklahoma. His short fiction and essays have appeared in a variety of magazines including *The Laurel Review, Short Story, Kansas Quarterly, The Chariton Review, Beloit Fiction Journal, The Florida Review, The Maryland Review, South Dakota Review*, and *Natural Bridge*. He is the author of two collections, ***SPYING ON LOVERS*** and ***WEDLOCK,*** and the novel ***LOVE AND RERUNS IN ADAMS COUNTY***. In addition to The Omaha Prize, he has been the recipient of The Patrick T. T. Bradshaw Book Award and The Faulkner Society Faulkner Award for Fiction.